D0357386

Praise for Bae Suah

"Bae Suah offers the chance to unknow—to see the everyday afresh and be defamiliarized with what we believe we know—which is no small offering."
—*Music & Literature*

"With concise, evocative prose, Bae merges the mundane with the strange in a way that leaves the reader fulfilled yet bewildered, pondering how exactly the author managed to pull this all off."
—*_list: Books from Korea*

"A compact, personal account of anomie and withdrawal in a time of rapid social and economic change. . . . An easily digested short book that nevertheless feels much very substantial—a very full story. Impressive, and well worthwhile."
—*The Complete Review*

"The mystery, like the achievement of [*Nowhere to Be Found*], occurs not in space, but in time."
—*The National*

also
by Bae
Suah

*Nowhere to
Be Found*

Translated from
the Korean by
Deborah Smith

Bae
Suah

A
Greater
MUSIC

OPEN LETTER
LITERARY TRANSLATIONS FROM THE UNIVERSITY OF ROCHESTER

Copyright © Bae Suah, 2003
Translation copyright © Deborah Smith, 2016
This English edition is published by arrangement with Munhakdongne Publishing Corp.

First edition, 2016
All rights reserved

Library of Congress Cataloging-in-Publication Data: Available.
ISBN-13: 978-1-940953-46-5 | ISBN-10: 1-940953-46-4

Printed on acid-free paper in the United States of America.

Text set in Garamond, a group of old-style serif typefaces
named after the punch-cutter Claude Garamont.

Design by N. J. Furl

Open Letter is the University of Rochester's nonprofit, literary translation press:
Lattimore Hall 411, Box 270082, Rochester, NY 14627

www.openletterbooks.org

A Greater MUSIC

G reater music,
the voice said. The voice governed the whole world under 3
the rain-streaked, cloud-wreathed sky. Dense with moisture, the
air pressed in through the open car window, forming droplets on
M's right cheek and the exposed side of her hair. M and I wanted
to listen to the sound of the rain falling on the fields. The rain-
water trickled down M's pale, almost ghost-like forehead, down
over her eyelids, still more sunken after her recent cold, and over
her slightly downward-pointing nose. When she tilted her head
upward, her lips appeared unbelievably thin and delicate, tapering
elegantly even when she wasn't smiling, flushed red as though suffused by the morning sunlight. The delicate, languidly prominent
scaffolding of her cheekbones, the cheekbones for which they had
teased her at school, saying they were like an Eskimo's; the muscles
directly below them trembled momentarily as if in a spasm. Far
over the fields, lightning flashed slowly. If books and language were
the symbol of M's absolute world, then music was her inaccessible

mind, her religion, her soul. We were descending the low-lying hills on which the rain was quietly falling. On both sides of the hills lay mown fields. The edge of the black woods was receding over them, but it was impossible to tell whether these woods existed in reality or were merely a shadow cast over the ground by the rain-laden clouds. That morning I'd stopped by the government office to sort out an issue with some documents. Before that, M had gone to get her doctor's permission to go on a short trip. Up until her death a week ago, M's aunt had been living in the city's outer ring, and M and I had decided to go and collect her things. M made no comment when Shostakovich came on. Greater music, said the voice on the radio. That recorded voice always reaches us after a certain lag, like the light from distant stars; the precise span of its existence in the world remained unknown. All we could do was listen, though what we heard didn't always correspond to the absolute value—the modulus, m—of existence. Nevertheless, without music, what kind of meaning could existence have? Greater music, saying "the voice" is surely more honest, rather than endowing it with the concrete weight of a human individual. When I heard those words on the radio it never occurred to me to personify the voice as "he" or "she." Greater, greater music, the voice said. The word "greater," which usually describes a comparison, isn't appropriate in this instance. The voice used "greater music" as an expression like greater beauty or greater sadness, greater distance, greater pain, greater solitude. More x-adjective music. We never say "greater death," death being an absolute value that does not admit comparison. Like one's hand, which can be flipped to show either the back or the palm, it's something that can only exist as one of two possibilities. Music is absolute, just like death. Just as "greater death" or "lesser death" is a logical impossibility, so the same can be said of music, which is of the same order

4

as the soul. A comparison cannot be made between listening to Beethoven's Concerto no. 2 or no. 3 as if one were "lesser" and the other "greater." Similarly, if one were to listen to a single one of Beethoven's concertos three times in a row, or listen to three different concertos one after the other, it would make no sense to declare that one of these is greater and the other is lesser. Might it be possible to use "greater music" as a way of expressing music *as it is listened to*, rather than a mere list of musical works? Can a word that expresses either something still more musical, a still deeper thirst for music (persisting in spite of much contemporary dross), or simply music itself, contain within itself the possibility for the many meanings that it connotes and suggests to be further amplified, to be somehow greater? Can it permit its own territory to be ambiguous, bounded by a far horizon incapable of clear demarcation? Greater music. Where might such words come from? The voice never made any association between Beethoven's Concerto no. 2 and no. 3. Perhaps, all things considered, "music is greater *to me*" might be a more appropriate expression. Greater death, greater nakedness (as opposed to an increased number of individual naked bodies), a more primordial human (but only one individual), a greater universe, the soul of greater music, a greater rarity, a greater distance from the present location, greater Mendelssohn, greater M, and that greater winter.

In the beginning there are memories. Conventional memories whose essence is either visual or aural, shifting eventually to those which, through their own agency, reclaim past scenes inside remembered soundscapes. Mendelssohn-Bartholdy-Strasse, immersed in the music I am oblivious to the fact that the train that I have to take has already pulled in, the passengers have already boarded and the train has whisked them away. Clara Schumann's portrait

5

gleaming pale above paper money, the Shostakovich corner in the LP store, a gramophone discovered in an antiques store on the craftsman's street, a museum of musical instruments down a small side street not marked on the map, music schools. More music. Raindrops fell, and were overlaid above with more drops, and above them still more. They fell continuously, layer upon layer, and an instinctive lifting of one's gaze sees severally existing worlds unfurl over the fields, stretching away beyond the gray barrier that marked the edge of the motorway. Air heavy with rain, overcast with clouds, churned by gusting wind, the melancholy color of a seemingly shadowed evening, earth and water and air and color. Of all the discrete chords pursuing infinite freedom each on their separate path, each in possession of their own language, a musician singled out one. That chord, which layered raindrop over raindrop, extended the domain of the original droplet throughout the world that lay beneath the massing clouds, beyond the fields and low hills and what had at one time been wilderness. On stage, at an orchestral concert I'd attended with M, an oboist mistakenly played a sharp note. It had happened at least twice by the time they were halfway through the movement, which wasn't a particularly long one. Overall, a disappointing performance. During the break, people milled around in the hall, wineglasses full. The sound of the wine lapping against the delicate glasses differed according to whether it was white or red. People in black woolen clothes gathered there, the sounds of their conversation filling the lower part of the cavernous space like smoke dispersing at a low height, before being gradually absorbed into the walls and portraits. This was in the dead of winter. It was at M's house that I first heard "At the Santé Prison," the song of a condemned man awaiting death. Between one piece and another, or one movement and another movement, I would open the kitchen window a little

6

and breathe in the crisp air, or make some fresh coffee. At first I was bored, unable to lose myself in the music. At the time I was more taken up with M than I was with Shostakovich. All the same, we listened to all fifteen of Shostakovich's symphonies, one after another, in no particular order. Symphony no. 11, Symphony no. 7, Symphony no. 14, Opus 135, the poetry of Lorca, Apollinaire, Rilke, Küchelbecker. The solo begins, death is omnipotent, without solace, afterimage, or praise. But before the song was over I'd left La Santé, no, M's house, and was heading home. The symphony had made an immediate impression on me. Later, I realized that it had caused me to acknowledge the omnipotence of death, the sole theme of such music. This acknowledgement hurt those close to me, and I had to endure their condemnation. The night was deep, the lamps stood unlit, and the paved road was uneven; the tram stop was some way off. Beneath the raindrops, still more raindrops were falling, not at a constant speed, but continuously. Beside them other raindrops were falling, also at unappointed intervals, and beside them still more raindrops, and beside them still more . . . thus was the world beneath the massed clouds captured and occupied. It was the empire of a mathematics which, for all its exquisite detail, was freed from the strictures of an orderly rhythm, and played extempore.

It was in my teens, when I got my own stereo and learned to play the piano and violin, that I found my way into the world of music. It was learning an instrument that opened this door, providing a deeper understanding than can be gained through passive listening. And yet I turned out to be utterly devoid of musical talent, even allowing for the fact that I was too old, by then, to be able to tap into that innate ear for music that children supposedly have. At the time, though, I can't say I really felt the lack, because in those days I imagined that this thing, music, was merely incidental to the world, a kind of garnish. In other words, I considered it on-par with overly embellished old-fashioned clothes, romantic poetry, my weekly art class, an intricately crafted dessert, the occasional trip to the theater as a reward for good grades. I was painfully sensitive as a teenager, at the mercy of the emotions that roiled and raged within me. The music lessons bored me, so I quit—that was the way I used to act, and I'm genuinely ashamed to think of it now. I was far more interested in other, "popular" things—films, music, dance—whose mind-numbing, facile simplicity meant they could be enjoyed without any form of critical engagement. My parents didn't know much about music themselves, and when I decided to drop my lessons in favor of learning a computer programming language, they agreed that this would be a more productive use of my time. After all, it wasn't as though I was intending to go on to music school, and the lesson fees hadn't exactly been cheap. My adolescence was marred with so much that was base and contemptible. In those days I had a Fischer-Dieskau record, ones by Maria Anderson and Maria Callas, and a Schubert collection (the name of the singer escapes me), as well as full-length aria collections like *Madame Butterfly* and *La Traviata*, etc. But I soon set aside that kind of music in favor of ABBA records, or the soundtracks of the latest popular films, which I borrowed from my classmates. At the time, the thing which dominated my life was neither films nor my father, but deference to the tastes and opinions of the group. Even then, I knew that *La Traviata* or Fischer-Dieskau were more beautiful than ABBA, but if I didn't listen to ABBA then I couldn't join in when my classmates enthused over their favorite songs. If I didn't watch the films that were constantly on at the theater, with their slick editing and predictable plots, then when all the other kids could talk of nothing else I would have to pretend I just hadn't gotten around to seeing it for some reason, and pay close attention while the others went on about how great it had been. Even worse would have been if I were to mention a scene from *La Traviata*, or praise Fischer-Dieskau's voice; then, as instantaneously as a trap snapping shut, I would be ostracized, deliberately ignored, my very existence blanked out. Adolescence is a time of uncertainty and instability, and I couldn't help but fear being condemned as old-fashioned, or as putting on airs. Worse, nothing that I learned at school gave me cause to suspect that there might be something more worthwhile than the simple, sentimental connection afforded by popular music. Being yourself was frowned upon, while ignorance was actively promoted. In those days, the authority of school was so absolute that neither I nor even my parents would dare to harbor thoughts that went against the grain. Such a thing would have been seen as undermining the good of the group, of which we were merely constituent parts. Of course, the teachers were ostensibly the ones who held the school under their sway, but they were merely the kings of the day, while the kings of the underground, the sovereigns of all darkness and terror, the merciless kings who dispensed with reason and logic, the brutal monarchs whose lust for fresh victims had all the hunger of a school of sharp-toothed piranhas, who would on no account allow their prey to go free until they were sated; they, the kings of night, already bearing in large part the natural disposition of the mob, and having this cultivated day by day, the anti-educators, were none other than the pupils.

Such a lot of time has gone by since then. Now, I have willingly taken upon myself the role of M's protector. An inconceivably intense affection flooded through me for the tender, haughty being known as M. I closed the glass window, anxious about the prospect of M catching yet another cold. The sharp tang of petrol pervaded the interior of the old car. M had a serious allergy to many medicines, so she couldn't take general fever remedies. Greater music, the voice said. Even before the final bar had ended, the voice repeated those same sounds, greater music. Like the raindrops which fell continuously, but seemingly without any fixed pattern, greater music, in an uncalculated extempore moment before the final notes were over, like the falling of the next raindrop while the lingering notes of the first still sound, falling to the ground beneath the clouds with no set beat, greater music, the next first notes joined the continuum. That continuous sound is called music. In winter.

Shostakovich's Sonata for Viola and Piano is his final work, which he completed while in the hospital. He seemed to have had a strong premonition regarding his own death. According to him: We don't simply fear death now and then; rather, our mortal lives are far more deeply threaded with its presence. At least, that's how it seems to me . . .

2) When I first fell into the water, although I was perfectly aware that this was all really happening, it felt as though I was still stuck inside a dream. I'm walking along the road, lifting my feet with that sluggishness found in dreams, that heaviness caused by the water sloshing inside my rain boots. Neither sadness, fear, nor despair, but gravity, endless and immense, has taken hold of me. I'm wandering between the houses, their numbers painted on white signs. I must be lost. It seemed I'd experienced brutal acts but could no longer remember them. No, I was simply struck by the sense of memory's intangibility, torn between struggling

to recall certain events as something concrete, and the instinct to leave them safely in the nebulous past. But such dreams were nothing new for me, and I didn't need to fight against the confusion; to a certain extent I actually enjoyed it. Even as the surface of the water broke my fall, I wasn't afraid. I saw pots of limp geraniums on a windowsill, the white drapes drawn, glass dolls with scarily large pupils, and green Christmas candles. I waved. As firecrackers snapped in the middle of the road, a yellow tram went by. Benny ran barking along the water's edge, where early bluebells bloomed between patches of unmelted snow. Nothing's the matter, Benny. This is only a dream. But no sound emerged from my throat. Benny was barking even louder. He ran into the wood that grew by the water, gradually speeding up so that in the end he was nothing but a blurry white ball, revolving with the world's axis as its center. What could have happened to upset him? I wanted to comfort him. My love, everything's alright. Just wait there and I'll come right back. There's a good boy, my love. But Benny couldn't hear me and streaked away, passing beyond my sight. Then the incongruous figure of a postman dressed all in yellow joined the scene. He'd parked his bicycle by the side of the road and was pressing the doorbell, holding the letters in one hand. There's no one home, so he'll just stick the letters in the mailbox; just as I was thinking this, I felt the first stab of the cold water, piercing the top of my head and the nape of my neck and the rim of my ears. The next moment I felt the weight of the water pull me under, cold hands seizing me and tugging me down. The cold was lethal, and my limbs were rapidly becoming numb. I'd fallen into the water, I knew this perfectly well, yet I kept on mechanically lifting my feet up and down. I imagined that I was walking down a flight of stairs—stairs of water, which were rapidly extending downward as I placed my feet on the next step. Without needing to look behind me, I knew that they were disappearing as I descended, that the section I'd passed had already dissolved into the water. The thought suddenly came to me that "returning" is merely a word, not something referring to a real possibility. I was going to mumble that something had gone wrong, but my frozen lips wouldn't part. Icy water had seeped in between them when I first fell in, freezing them into immobility after my initial cry of distress. Water bearing the deep chill of midwinter, water that pierces and penetrates warm winter clothes, cold enough to carry off my soul. A devil was stabbing me with an ice poker. When I broke the surface I'd felt a pain as though my lips had been gashed on sharp rocks, as though a bone had broken in my left side, so extreme that I saw fireworks flash in front of my eyes.

This is a dream, the continuation of a dream, I thought. This is a dream, and since it's a dream there's no need for me to struggle. Because that's the way it is with dreams, and because it was clear that, however much I struggled, my physical strength would be negligible at best. Yet I thrashed my limbs mercilessly all the same, and a bubbling sound escaped from between my lips. Although I'd stopped sinking, I was unable to free myself from my waterlogged coat and boots, which were weighing me down. Not much time had passed since I fell in, so the water had only come up to my forehead. I tried to swim, but I couldn't get my body to move in the way I ordered it. Fear of suffocation was rapidly paralyzing me. Convinced that my heavy boots were what was dragging me down, I made a foolish attempt to remove them and got a mouthful of water for my pains. I floundered, choking, tried to float on the surface, tried again to remove my boots, and eventually I discovered myself thinking "this is a dream," and letting everything take its own course as my body sank weakly into the water. How could I have fallen in? I mean, how could I be unwittingly wearing a warm coat with two sweaters and a hat, woolen socks, jeans and rain boots? It hadn't even been a minute since I'd fallen in, but it felt so much longer. My strength had faded, there was absolutely nothing I could do any more. I didn't even have the strength to move my little finger. That was when the word death first came into my mind, as did the thought that I was lucky not to have been sentenced to death; somewhat incongruous given that, as far as I could remember, I'd never committed a crime that would warrant such a punishment. The mere mention of capital punishment was enough to send a shiver through me, as though I were undergoing some terrible humiliation. To me, capital punishment, administered in full accordance with an established legal system, seemed even more humiliating than a public flogging. Being murdered had always seemed immensely preferable to the ordeal of capital punishment. Death; until now it had always been something to do with other, far-away people, but now it was all too intimate. Although I tried to tell myself that it was something I just had to accept, that after all this was only a dream, it was all too evident that I was suffocating. Confusion slowly changed into humiliation as I realized that I was going to experience both a basic agony and an inexhaustible humiliation.

To M as much as to me, it simply wasn't possible that I would die first of the two of us. Such thoughts had even escaped her lips, and on more than one occasion. This assumption was hardly unreasonable considering the parade of illnesses, both major and minor, that had been M's adolescence, the three operations she'd had so far, and the hereditary allergy which threatened to flare up whenever she strayed too far from her familiar environment. It was so much a part of her life that she barely even noticed it any more, living hemmed in by the many medicines which she had to take, the doctors' addresses, the phone calls to book appointments. M's allergy caused her unimaginable suffering, so much so that, she told me, she'd once decided to kill herself rather than bear it any longer. The doctors were all of the opinion that M's other disorders of the nervous system were triggered by this allergy. Even though these weren't life-threatening, whenever I thought of death it had become a habit to think of it connection with M. M knew this perfectly well. But how foolish I'd been to think that way—now M would have no reason to hate or envy me any more, as she was going to outlive me. But there was no way she'd ever be able to learn the details of my death. She would never know about the humiliation, and this was all that was needed to set my mind at ease.

Death, being unaware that one is no longer living. Strangely enough, after that thought surfaced in my mind, the pain seemed gradually to lessen in intensity. Like so many other things that get forgotten in this world, the feeling as though my lungs were bursting slowly lost its original character, becoming "pain" only in name, a pain that was "mine" yet felt strangely disconnected. I was lying on the water. I wasn't floating perfectly, though; I was lying on my side facing the riverbank, repeatedly sinking beneath the surface only to float up again a few moments later. I could gulp down a quick breath if I twisted my head when I floated up, but this was getting progressively more difficult. I knew I had to tilt my head up so I could breathe, but I was so weak that I frequently just sank straight back down again. My legs were starting to weigh me down, dragging me back under. The pain in my side remained constant all the while, but it now felt less like pain and more like evidence of some irreversible severing or fatal decision in the midst of this slow death. I was conscious of the sensation that we call "pain," but it wasn't the least bit painful any more. Eventually, like my inability to breathe, it became both the sole thing left to define me and my final farewell to this world, the total sum of my existence.

3) We'd arranged to go to Joachim's house on Christmas Eve. His mother's house, to be precise. I was also planning to attend a midnight church service, though for architectural rather than religious reasons. The area where his mother lived was nothing special but, according to Joachim, it had a particularly beautiful church. His family was Protestant, but Joachim hadn't been to church for a very long time. It wasn't snowing on the morning of Christmas Eve, but the snow that had fallen the night before hadn't completely melted, leaving the roads churned with dirty slush and snow still piled up on the pavements. The wind was so strong it swept up snow from the unmelted piles and scattered it into the air. Joachim had been in a bad mood all day, perhaps because of the imminent family gathering. In fact, he'd wanted to skip the whole thing, catch a bus straight from the airport to the train station, then jump on the first train to Schleswig-Holstein. But I didn't have the money for yet another trip, and besides, several years ago I'd gone on holiday to East Asia over Christmas, so I knew what a bad idea it was to travel at that time of year. All the tourist attractions are closed, and the only thing haunting the deserted streets is your own solitary shadow. In the mornings, while you spread subway tickets out on the table at the guesthouse, after breakfast and coffee; while reading the information boards in a woodland park that seems once to have been a mountaintop castle, strewn with the wreckage of broken armaments or the detritus of some bygone aristocratic hunt; while browsing the Christmas market in the square; at all times, and in all places, your thoughts revolve

15

solely around deciding where to visit next. But then, I'd known in advance that it would be like that, that everything would be desolate and I would end up wandering around on foot, shivering in the cold. In fact, I came to realize that the 1,500 kilometers I'd traveled had only served to further the distance between myself and my original goal. It was a goal that simply could not be attained. I struggled to explain to Joachim about that holiday to the East. That holiday of which I had never spoken to anyone, when I took the night train far away with heavy bags and a heavier heart, yet was ultimately unable to break free from myself. But Joachim just couldn't grasp what I was trying to say. "What on earth is that supposed to mean? 'Break free from myself,' you mean like dying or going crazy? So your holiday was pointless, I can't understand what that has to do with Christmas. And besides, Schleswig-Holstein isn't exactly East Asia, is it?" This wasn't entirely unreasonable; right up until our last goodbye, I'd been dreaming of traveling to the north. But not now. After breakfast we take our dog Benny for a walk. The sun is shining through a gap in the clouds though, as usual, the cold wind makes our skin feel tight. We walk in silence, along the same route we always take. Sometimes Benny stops to have a sniff around, and if he catches a scent or just absent-mindedly flops down on the ground, we stop walking too, and stare at the wood of denuded larches, their outlines stark and bare. In the wood there is a small lake, completely frozen over at this time of year. People go there to skate. We walk over the frozen lake. Benny barks nervously as soon as we step out onto the ice, perhaps disliking the cold, slippery sensation beneath his feet, and speeds off to the far bank. Heeding Benny's distrust of the ice, we decide against crossing the lake and stroll around the edge instead, watching the skaters. Joachim doesn't have a jacket, so is wrapped up in two sweaters, a hat and a black muffler. At times he looks more like a

"Peter" than a "Joachim." My love. Joachim calls Benny in a low voice. My love, stay. We're coming right back. Good boy, my love. We walked up and down, having assured ourselves that the lake ice was solid and not likely to break. Snow had erased the contours of the paths through the wood, rendering them indistinguishable from the surroundings, but the footprints of people and their dogs were outlined sharp against the whiteness. Wild rose bushes hung with small, hard, red fruit formed a low hedge, and every time the wind blew the high, snow-laden branches quivered and creaked ominously. Hulking crows perched on ice-covered branches that glittered silver when struck by the low, slanting rays of the winter sun. Soon, though, swiftly gathering clouds obscured all traces of its presence in the sky. It looked as though it would snow again that evening. Joachim was walking about three or four paces ahead of me. He said that if he'd known how to skate he would have borrowed a pair and gone out onto the ice right now. I'd learned how to skate when I was eleven, I told him, but that it was so long ago that I wasn't sure whether I would remember how, and besides, it was so cold right now that I wasn't thinking about anything at all. We resumed our silent walk. We felt the cold stab of the air entering our lungs as a physical impact, and if we coughed the steam of our breath came out white. I asked Joachim if he was cold without a coat, but he just shrugged in reply. When we came up to the lake caretaker's hut, a humble shack made of yellow bricks and wood, he suggested that we'd walked for long enough now and might as well head home. We found Benny waiting for us at the hut, fixing us with his faithful stare, almost as if he feared that we might disappear if he didn't keep us in sight. The return trip was colder than the way out. I was all but running. We decided that it was too cold to walk all the way, and took the tram. Benny's dislike of the tram was plain, but he flattened his body to lie obediently under the seat when Joachim told him to. Every time Benny jerked his head up, clearly ill at ease, Joachim produced a dog biscuit from his pocket and held it out to him. Benny would then settle down again, bury his face under the seat and chew his biscuit. The thought only then occurring to me, I asked Joachim if he'd bought a present for his parents. "A book and some perfume," he replied briefly, adding that he hadn't bought anything for his brother.

"In that case I guess I can get something for him."

Joachim assured me there was no need, although I suggested that going empty handed to a Christmas dinner made me feel uncomfortable.

"Besides, you can't," he grinned. "All the shops will be closed now, you know. I mean, where are you going to get a present from?"

In that case there was nothing to be done. We went home, Joachim ironed a shirt to wear that evening, and I made a simple Chinese noodle dish for lunch. After I boiled the water for the noodles according to the instructions, scooped them out with a sieve and drained them, I fried them in the big wok together with a jar of bean sprouts. According to Joachim the wok had been a real bargain, something he'd gotten off his friend's Vietnamese neighbor. Once the noodles heated through, I dished them up and finished them off with a sprinkle of salt, some garlic, and Thai chili sauce. The radio was playing Christmas songs back to back, many of them with practically the same melody, so we switched over to a news program, made some jasmine tea, and ate lunch. The tram rattled by outside. On the news we heard that the snow had caused many accidents on the motorways, and that there were floods in southern Germany. Once he'd finished the dishes, Joachim flopped down on the sofa, yawning, and began to browse one of his many train magazines—he couldn't get enough of them—while

I flicked through the television channels. The Christmas-themed programming was ubiquitous—Christmas carols, Christmas films, Christmas Mass, Christmas cooking, Christmas plays, Christmas discussions, etc. On the table there was a silver box of chocolates with some left over, and a book Joachim had been reading, *General Physics Theory with Mathematical Proofs*. He'd already passed the basic physics exam in his first term, but had apparently forgotten almost all of it and so was looking over it again. Benny was lying by Joachim's side; Joachim had the magazine in one hand and held Benny by the scruff of the neck with the other. The small, snow-covered road that ran through the backyard was visible through the high glass window. Lined with individual gardens known as "small gardens," it led to the local cemetery. The winter landscape was unchanging, and would remain so at least until the Christmas and New Year holidays were over. Every morning after breakfast we read a book, prepared something simple to eat, and watched some monotonous TV program; at night we listened to the radio, and three times a day we took Benny out for a short walk. In between that, we passed the time by doing the laundry, cleaning the bathroom, and taking the tram into town if there was something we needed to buy. Switching over to MTV, I stretched out on the bed, a wave of drowsiness surging over me. I'd barely gotten any sleep the previous night, having arrived at Joachim's in the early hours of dawn after a six-hour train journey. I'd flown into an airport outside Berlin, which meant two train changes with all my luggage, though Joachim had met me at the airport and helped carry the heavy bags. Arriving back in the city after a three-year absence, the first thing I saw was the night bus-stop near the station, in the falling snow. I sat on a suitcase while we waited for the bus; they came every half hour. The snow was falling heavily, too heavy for an umbrella or hat to be of much use. The roads had completely iced over because of the sudden drop in temperature. The train had been delayed by around two hours and after catching the bus we had to change again to take the tram. It was the Christmas holidays, and on top of it being late at night the snow was really coming down, so there were barely any passing cars even on the main road. The first thing that struck me was how unimaginably cold the bus stop was. That infinite, embalmed silence, the frozen torpor of the season, compounded by the extreme cold, pincered the heart in a viselike grip. Snow, rain, agonizing cold, the blank sky, the air heavy as if weighted down. Even when we got back to Joachim's and got into bed the cold still did not completely dissipate. The sound of the wind continued until morning, and until the sun trembled over the rim of the horizon, rising as cold as the thin layer of ice that rimmed the outside of the window, I couldn't shake myself free from the memory of the airplane's narrow seat, the continuous roaring of the engine, the vibration of the train as it rattled over the tracks. And so of course I was incredibly tired, and just as I was thinking to myself how tired I was, I fell asleep.

When I woke from sleep I was at a loss to say where I was. The room was so dark I assumed it was the middle of the night. It was completely silent, the curtains were drawn, and there was no sign of either Joachim or Benny. It had been a dreamless sleep. The only source of illumination was the light from the TV, showing a live broadcast of a performance by the Berlin Philharmonic. Karajan's face appeared on the screen. Only when I looked at the hands of the clock on the bedside table did I realize that I'd only slept for three hours. It was unusually dark for daytime; when I opened the curtains I saw that the whole city lay overshadowed by black clouds, from which the snow had slowly started to fall. The Berlin Phil was doing Rossini's *William Tell Overture*. Perhaps Joachim had changed the channel and left it on when he went out. Unfortunately, it was almost at the final movement, and after a brief commercial the program continued with Ravel's *Boléro*. I wasn't fond of the *Boléro*. It was a shame I hadn't woken up a little earlier, when the *William Tell Overture* was still on. I must have slept in an awkward position, because my right arm and my entire torso were tingling. I lay there in the bed and stared at the old ceiling. Originally there'd been an electric bulb suspended from it, but now all that was left was a short wire. Joachim had thought the light made the room too bright, so he'd pulled it out. As a replacement, he'd put a desk lamp on the small table that could be used for reading and writing, and there was a stand by the bed. The bookcase was filled with magazines and dictionaries, along with several volumes on physics and art theory—no different from when I first came here three years ago. Several old magazines had disappeared and been replaced by new ones, and the collection seemed to be missing several Baedeker guidebooks, plus two or three books on maths or physics which I remembered from before, but apart from that almost nothing had changed. Novels were represented solely by the English-language versions of the *Harry Potter Series* and *American Psycho*. Those were inside the wardrobe, where we'd put my suitcase yesterday. I opened it, took out my books, and put them on the bookshelves. I'd brought some translations of Dostoevsky with me, but I wouldn't be reading them here. I'd read them before, for one thing, though this had been some time ago, and had realized that reading them again would be tedious. I tried reading one on the plane, but had to put it aside. Joachim had more than enough magazines, so I tossed some into the wastepaper basket to make room for my books. After Christmas I would have to go into the city center to buy some more. Cookbooks or animal photo albums; classics which I'd read a long time ago but had forgotten both the plot and the significance, in fact everything but the title; twentieth-century contemporary history; postwar history; war crimes trials; or essays about the deaths of musicians. I'd always liked reading, but over the past few years I'd thrown myself into it with increasing gusto. One reason was that I'd begun to spend the vast majority of my time alone. I went into the kitchen to make coffee. The small fridge was packed, as Joachim had said. He'd stocked up on all sorts of groceries just before the start of the Christmas shopping wars. Two bags of coffee, an easy-bake Christmas cake and a bottle of milk, frozen spinach and other vegetables, honey and butter, bread and eggs, apples and red cabbage for cooking in pig fat, a jar of bean sprouts and a packet of Chinese noodles. The kitchen window looked out directly onto the road to the cemetery. At the entrance to the road, affixed to the wall of the building directly beneath the kitchen, a lamp gave off a yellow glow. Snowflakes swirled and streamed, glittering like shards of glass in that light.

Joachim came home. In the hallway he brushed off the snow that was stuck to Benny's fur, and took off his jacket. He didn't much like that old, threadbare jacket, and would only put it on if he thought it was going to be extremely cold. He sat at the small kitchen table and I poured him some of the coffee I'd made. After that we began to wrap the presents he'd bought. He'd bought a cookbook for his mother and an eau de cologne for his father. He apologized that he hadn't been able to get anything for me, but that was only to be expected, since I'd only told him I was coming a couple of days ago. The day was now as dark as the depths of night, and the sound of the gusting wind could be heard through the shuddering windows. The falling snow swirled through the air, practically a blizzard. Joachim said we'd best wear scarves and gloves. And hats too, I added. He took a chocolate from the box he'd carried into the room, gave it to Benny, and took another for himself. When he'd finished eating it, chewing slowly like a man deep in thought, he picked out another piece. I asked if he wanted me to make him some bread and honey, but he shook his head and fetched a big tub of Nutella from the cupboard, which he'd bought on sale. He got out a knife and a plate and began to slather the chocolate on the bread I'd given him. Benny watched this process with a look of great interest, wagging his tail all the while. The kitchen only had one small light, fixed directly above the dishwasher. Yellow light from the wall lamp further down the side of the building streamed up and illuminated the whirling snowstorm outside the window. After taking a sip of coffee Joachim opened his mouth wide and bit off a chunk of the chocolate-covered bread. He didn't give any to Benny, who waited patiently nonetheless. "Did you bring boots?" Joachim asked. "If you didn't, your feet'll get soaked. That's how bad this snow is." I'd only brought one pair of shoes with me; rain boots, as luck would have it. I took off Joachim's pajamas, which I'd slept in, and found a pair of jeans to put on. I put a sweater on over my T-shirt, pulled on some thick woolen socks and went into the bathroom to comb my hair. The kitchen door stood open and through it I could see Joachim polishing off the rest of the bread, muttering to himself all the while. When our eyes met he raised his eyebrows as if to say, what's the hurry?, and carried on slowly chewing the bread, staring up at the ceiling with his body stretched out in the chair. I stood beside the front door and waited quietly until he'd finished getting ready. Benny saw the clothes Joachim was wearing and gave a short, sharp bark, angry at being left behind. But there was nothing to be done. My love. Joachim put his arms around Benny's neck and soothed him, kissing him again and again. My love, you have to stay here quietly. You wait here and I'll be back before you know it. Good boy, my love.

23

When we left the house the blizzard had abated somewhat, but the wind was as strong as ever. It was already completely dark. We began to walk silently along the snow-covered road toward the light at the tram stop. Joachim walked in front, carrying a blue backpack into which he'd stuffed the presents. It was the selfsame backpack I remembered from three years ago, and even back then it had already been pretty old. Now it had holes in the bottom, big enough to be instantly noticeable. I was a little surprised that he was still using it. I could see that the snow had soaked through the tops of his thin sneakers, and his feet were getting wet. His thin, light-colored jeans flapped around his skinny shins as he hurried along. When we arrived at the tram stop we brushed ourselves off and checked the timetable.

"We'll have to wait twenty minutes or so. What shitty luck," Joachim grumbled. We were the only people waiting there. On the opposite platform there were two young children and one woman, standing stock-still and bundled up in bulky winter clothes like an Inuit family. In an attempt to ward off the tedium and the cold, I turned my attention to the various notices pinned up on the board and gave them a thorough examination. There was an ad for beer that made my teeth chatter just looking at it. Except for a family play, an exhibition of paintings, an exhibition of ancient relics classified by cultural-anthropological periods, and large business ads, they were all advertising New Year's fireworks parties. There was also something about writers giving a public reading at the town's only café. Joachim tapped his finger on the place where it said "free admission."

"Want to go?"

I said I wasn't sure. A cup of coffee would set me back at least two euros, and I couldn't make a single cup last for over two hours, but then if we ordered beer or something that would make it too expensive. Plus, there would be a fee for the brochure. But, more than anything else, I really didn't feel like going out anywhere, not while the weather was still like this. It was just too cold.

"I think I'd rather just stay home and read a book."

"Sure, whatever you want," Joachim said. "When the weather gets better you should go to the library and use my card. That's free, after all. And maybe we'll get to go to a party for New Year's, have some wine. Also, when you said you were coming I booked us tickets for the Philharmonic's New Year concert. Lucky there were still some seats left."

"Wasn't it expensive?"

"A bit. And I wasn't sure if it's the kind of thing you like. It's choral music, you see. Probably Mozart and Beethoven's masses."

"I don't mind."

"Do you have any dress clothes? If not, you can always call one of your girlfriends and ask to borrow something."

"Don't worry about it, I brought something with me."

All I'd brought was a jacket with a stiff collar and some woolen trousers that were slightly stretched at the knees, but I figured they would be good enough. We stood there shivering in silence until the tram pulled in. The snow, which had somehow found its way in through our hats and scarves, formed droplets of icy water and trickled down to the napes of our necks. It was a Christmas of freezing temperatures and driving snow. Identical rectangular houses lined both sides of the road, impassive as soldiers on a midwinter battlefield. The tram passed along the tracks between them, between those houses where curtains hung in the windows and Christmas decorations glittered on candlelit balconies. Three years ago I often got lost here, as there was no way to tell the buildings apart unless you checked the house numbers. On top of that, the area was completely devoid of any kind of landmark, even so much

25

as a shop with a sign. But I didn't lose heart even when I realized I was lost, just continued to walk along the same road. Turning to the left, there's a vacant lot that the locals use as a dump. Large iron bins stand beside flowerbeds. Even in that vacant patch of ground, yellow wildflowers bloom in the spring. Continuing on, the quiet road comes to a sudden end and a very different scene unfolds: a large T-junction appears with trams running along the crisscrossing tracks, each going in different directions. On the corner is a Turkish kebab shop; in the summer, when the weather is good, the shop is given a fresh coat of paint, dazzlingly white, and tables and chairs are set out on the tiny patch of grass that forms the yard, and they sell beer and lamb skewers. I've never gone into the shop, even though I've walked down this road many times from summer to late autumn, but I always notice it standing there, gleaming like something seen in a dream. Of course, now that it's winter the shop is closed. On the opposite side of the road is the path leading to the lake, where Joachim takes Benny for walks. If you turn right again, white signposts stand in rows, bearing the house numbers of the identical military buildings, themselves a light green color like soldiers in summer uniform. On both sides of the road the scene that presents itself is so orderly, so repetitive, that it's almost uncanny. Somewhere among this order is a narrow road leading behind the buildings, adorned with small rectangular gardens. Now, the apple trees and western pear trees, the small artificial lotus ponds, and the brick flower beds all lie under a thick covering of snow. If you follow those small gardens the road leads to the cemetery. Joachim lives on the second floor of the corner building. The first time I came to his house it was around dusk, and the darkness had a reddish tinge as if the landscape had rusted. Alighting from the tram, he'd gestured toward the strange, silent, red-tinted road and said "Welcome to the ghetto."

26

When we arrived they were already sitting gathered in front of the television in the living room, with the window open, sipping cappuccinos while watching a Christmas special. Joachim's mother Agnes and her boyfriend Bjorn, and Joachim's twin brother Peter. Joachim headed into the living room and slumped down into a spare place on the sofa, without so much as a single word of greeting. As soon he sat down he opened the TV listings magazine, a double edition for Christmas, and started to go through it. Agnes and Bjorn said hello to me. When I'd visited Agnes briefly three years ago, she'd had a different boyfriend. And I'd never met Peter before. Joachim had never even spoken all that much about him. I'd thought they might be identical twins, but I could see now that they weren't.

"Cappuccino?" Agnes asked, getting up from her seat. I nodded and thanked her. "How was your trip?" Bjorn asked, turning to look at me.

"It was okay. But the constant rain meant we couldn't go outside much."

"Oh, it rained? Here we've just had snow."

When he laughed he let his mouth open wide. Peter's gaze was fixed on the television screen as if there was something gluing it there. He greeted me only briefly, his hello stiff and formal. He didn't look at Joachim and Joachim didn't look at him, but then Joachim didn't look at anything—he just sat there selecting chocolates from a glass dish on the side table, peeling off the silver paper and popping them into his mouth one at a time, with his face buried in the TV guide. A violinist appeared on the television and began to run through a series of popular Christmas pieces, his features arranged in an expression of generic happiness.

"André Rieu, there's really no one like him," Agnes sighed, gazing at the television while she settled back down on the sofa. "Don't you agree?" she asked me. "He's so attractive, and the music is just wonderful, don't you think?"

"I'm sorry?" I asked. I hadn't quite caught the name. "Who are you talking about?"

"André Rieu, the violinist. He has his own orchestra. He's Dutch."

"I've never heard of him."

The violinist was clearly putting a lot of effort into his facial expression and body language; no matter what he was playing, that happy smile never left his face. While he played he moved elegantly about the stage, making sure to hold the violin at a graceful angle. His long curly hair was pulled back with a stylish purple hair-tie, and each of his on-stage gestures were carefully calculated for a specific effect, like those of a gifted actor. Agnes gestured toward a shelf of books.

"I've got an André Rieu album—photos, you know."

"Oh?" I tried to sound polite rather than genuinely enthusiastic in case she suggested I have a look through the album, which I'd spotted next to a large, thick volume entitled *Princess Diana: Her Glory and Myth*. But then my gaze landed on something else, on the same shelf as the books: a black and white photograph in a small, finely carved wooden frame. It was a waist-up photograph of a young woman; it appeared to be quite an old picture, and the woman to be around fifteen. She was wearing a dark dress, probably black, and her blonde hair was tied back; it gave the impression of having been taken to mark a special occasion. A handful of pale-cultured roses were clutched to her chest, and her lips were curved into a smile that was both delicate and sharp, matching the contours of her face. The girl was standing in front of what looked like the door to a building. Her face looked pale and drawn for one so young. Overall, the impression was of a strange combination of cunning and freshness, of time flowing past in water. There was no question about it—this was Agnes, a long time ago. All the same I asked Joachim:

"Is this a photo of Agnes?"

"How would I know?" he responded brusquely, without even glancing at the photograph.

After the meal, when Agnes had finished the dishes and came to join the rest of us in the living room, I pointed out the photograph on the shelf and asked if it was a photo of her.

"Yes, that's right. It's a photo of the old days."

"Agnes, you were really pretty."

"There's no need to lie," Joachim said, without looking at me.

"It's not a lie, it's true. How old were you?"

"I was thirteen. 1963. The day of my First Communion. That's an important day in the Protestant church, you know."

"So that's why you were wearing those fancy clothes? The black dress?"

"That's why I wore the black dress, yes. And the roses were a gift."

"Were they white?"

"Hmm, no, they weren't white. I can't remember all that well. Were they yellow, maybe? Just a minute."

She disappeared into the bedroom and came back with a big cardboard box. Joachim tossed aside the magazine he'd been reading with an expression of annoyance, and Peter stubbed out his cigarette in the ashtray, keeping his eyes on the television. From the box, Agnes produced a headband that looked as though it hadn't been worn for years. "The very same," she said, indicating the one in the photograph. The box also contained a thick, black album, the photos glued to its thin white pages. They were all scenes from weddings. On the first page was a young Agnes, dressed in a pale two-piece and wearing cat-eye glasses. The man standing at her side was a little shorter than her, had clear, pale skin, and hair styled into the same shape as a sailor's cap. Agnes explained that this was in the government office, right after the wedding ceremony. "That was my first wedding," she added, reaching out to take the glass of spirits Bjorn was offering her. Compared to the previous photograph, this Agnes had cheeks that could almost be called plump. It wasn't just her cheeks—her shoulders too, in fact her whole body was filled out nicely. She and the other women, who I guessed were her sisters, all had bouffant hairstyles and glasses of the same distinct shape, and were wearing two-pieces cut to the same pattern. I recognized the style, having seen similar things in photos of my mother when she was young. It was the style adopted by Jacqueline Kennedy when she was the wife of the American president. It was all very evocative of a certain distinct period, which I suppose must have been one of those historical moments where young women the world over got married in similar clothes. The wedding reception had been attended by Agnes's sisters, their husbands, and her older brothers, the men all in suits. They were young, every one of them, and incomparably beautiful; there was even something brave in their youth and their beauty. They were like flowers daring to bloom amid the ruins of a city devastated by war. Moreover, this was a city that seemed to have been a humble place of woods, lakes, and simple, unembellished houses. These women had nothing to obscure the bright freshness of their youth; no makeup, no accessories, not even any coquetry. The square in the city center was truly vast, and the wide, straight road looked as though it might well stretch all the way to distant Poland. On this road, flanked by a seemingly endless forest, people from all walks of life stood holding hands and smiling brightly. It was as if I could hear their laughter and their song.

"I was seventeen then. He became ill, afterward, and died."

"Do your siblings still live around here?"

"I'm not sure. We haven't seen each other for, oh, decades, now."

I wasn't sure how many times Agnes had been married, but in any case I was certain that the short man with the sailor-style hair, whom Agnes had married at seventeen, wasn't Joachim and Peter's father. Later, when simple curiosity prompted me to ask Joachim how many times his mother had been married, he picked a train magazine up off the sofa and tossed it swiftly over the side, snapping "thirty-three times." In the photographs of her first wedding, Agnes had been like a budding flower, swelling with fresh, ripe fullness. She no longer resembled the girl who, at thirteen, had posed for her First Communion photograph with a shy, wavering smile. Similarly, the image of Agnes at her first wedding, in a dress and thick-framed glasses, held no premonition as to what the future would hold—of the alcoholic who can't get to sleep unless she's had a drink at the local pub; of being constantly unemployed and with no hope of this changing, searching for neighborhoods where the rent is cheap; of the loneliness of the matchmaking party at the singles' club every weekend, desperate to find a man worth living with.

The night had grown late when Joachim and I got up to leave. We walked to the church, which may well have displayed surpassing architectural beauty, but as there was no source of light anywhere in the immediate vicinity I wasn't able to confirm this. Before we went in, Joachim asked if I had any money to put in the collection plate. Some loose change, I told him, but he said that wouldn't do; with it being Christmas, it had be a note of some kind. He opened his wallet and pulled out his last five-euro bill. The notice board listed the organ music that was to be used during the service. The church was packed with people, most of them elderly, although there were also plenty of families with children, including one young couple carrying a tiny baby in a small wicker basket. The organist had already started playing, the notes echoing loudly throughout the vaulted, stone-ceilinged space. At the entrance to the church was a model reproduction of the Bethlehem manger, fronted by countless glowing candles that made the scene bright and warm. In between the organ pieces were hymns for the congregation to sing, though I wouldn't have called it singing because they all seemed to be mumbling the words. As soon as Joachim entered the church and slid into the back pew he closed his eyes and rested his chin on his chest; he didn't answer when I spoke to him, and I guessed he must have fallen asleep. His blue backpack slid off and came to rest under the seat, between his legs. Someone behind me handed me a songbook, so I turned and thanked them. After the last notes from the organ had faded away, a man—presumably the priest—spoke into the microphone; I couldn't tell what he was saying over the screeching feedback. As soon as the congregation resumed their singing, Joachim's eyes snapped open. So he hadn't been asleep after all. And he hadn't been crying. Whatever he'd been doing, he'd been perfectly alert and listening to everything.

"Let's head off now, we've seen enough." He picked up his bag and slung it over his shoulder.

"You want to leave right now, while everyone's singing?"

"Yes, right now."

Entirely indifferent to the stares he was eliciting, Joachim stood up and headed quickly toward the exit. Emerging into the freezing night air, he opened his wallet with a triumphant flourish and drew out the same five-euro bill again. "I got to see the service, and I didn't even have to put this in the plate! If we'd waited until that song was over they would have sent the plate around and there'd have been no getting out of it then. That's what that guy up there said, with the microphone."

The snow had melted a little during the day but was now blanketing the road again. "We've made a mess of the climate," Joachim said as we stood waiting at the tram stop. "Don't you think? Think about this crazy snow every day, and the floods in the south. I mean, this is colder than the winter I spent working in Finland." Joachim put his backpack back on and wound his scarf tightly around his neck. Before starting college, he said, he'd spent a brief period working as a welder in Finland. "Even if the tram doesn't come because of the snow, we can always just jog home, you know. In fact, last autumn when there was a subway strike I walked more than three hours from Alexanderplatz to home. And this was after working all day, from 8 A.M. to 6 P.M. God, that was awful. It was a Thursday, and on Fridays I had to go to school, so you can imagine. To make matters worse, I had an exam that Friday, ha-ha-ha! Compared with back then, this snow is actually pretty light. If we walk home quickly we'll be able to get back within an hour. And you had enough to eat, right? How come you didn't have more of the meat? You need a full stomach to keep you warm if we're going to make our way home through a blizzard like this. You can stuff yourself with potatoes and cabbage and whatnot till your stomach explodes, but that won't do anything for you. Agnes gets 150 euros for me every month—150 euros, think about it. For that amount I could have hot soup and coffee every day for lunch at the college cafeteria, for a whole month! And she refused to hand it over. Money from the government that she only gets as maintenance for me. And now she says she won't give it to me—right after telling me I should come over to eat with them every weekend! But don't you think it's ridiculous, people who've done nothing but argue over money for a whole year, getting together just because it's Christmas, and putting on this charade of a solemn, harmonious family dinner? Well, we got a good meal out of it, anyway, and that means it's okay if we walk, right? I know the weather's rough, but do you think you can walk home all the same? The route's easy enough, we just need to keep following the tramline in the same direction. There's nothing to it. Ah, my family is a disgrace. I mean, seriously." Joachim babbled on, snickering to himself, but while he was still in full flow the yellow light of the approaching tram pierced the snowstorm. We were in luck. That night there was a sharp drop in temperature, so the entrances to the subway stations were left open for the homeless to take shelter there. According to Joachim, we would have had a truly terrible time if we'd had to walk. When I asked him later if he'd seriously been considering walking back, he said he'd just been babbling thoughtlessly, with no clear idea of the words that were coming out of his mouth, just to keep his lips from freezing.

4) The New Year's Eve party we ended up going to was hosted by Alfred, Joachim's fireman friend from technical college, at his house near North Berlin Fire Station. Alfred, who sported a neat goatee and owned a gaudy red leather jacket with gold trim, was unvaryingly cheerful, meaning he sometimes came across as quite shallow or flippant. He loved hosting parties and presiding over gatherings of friends, and always made sure to include Joachim even though he could be relied upon to turn up empty-handed, while everyone else would bring wine or cake. Alfred's magnanimity also extended to me; I'd been invited to a number of his parties in the past, and had made frequent promises to attend, which I then broke without exception. Alfred kept on

inviting me all the same. He mistook me for, variously: a current university student; someone from some other Asian country; and Joachim's ex-girlfriend. In fact, every time he met me Alfred could be relied upon to ask how I was in a way that made it clear that he thought I was someone else. However, neither Joachim nor I were particularly bothered by this, so we never felt the need to set him straight. Even though it wasn't snowing on New Year's Eve, I always hated having to venture outside when there could be fireworks going off in my face at any moment. Very occasionally, if Joachim had annoyed me, I would refuse to go. I really couldn't stand parties. But he was obsessed with showing me these so-called "student parties" (the only ones I'd been to had been held by foreigners), the kind where they play classic Oasis and Nirvana rather than crazy techno or American-style "butt dance" or hip-hop, and some of the students are Scandinavian, and they talk to each other in English. This was the kind of party Alfred generally went in for—in fact, he had a cousin who was Scandinavian—and Joachim had been eagerly awaiting the opportunity to prove to me that he himself was perfectly at home at such parties. Unfortunately, though, Alfred hadn't called up any Scandinavian friends this time; apparently they'd all gone back home for Christmas. Nirvana was blasting out of the computer speakers, but the music video kept stopping and the screen freezing, so the same music played on a loop for several hours. Apart from Alfred, the only other person there whom Joachim knew personally was a German literature major; he was very handsome, despite having a somewhat sly smile, but only had eyes for his new girlfriend, whom he'd met a week ago. He brushed Joachim off with an absent-minded greeting, and never left his girlfriend's side. It wasn't just because of his girlfriend, though. Contrary to Joachim's expectation, the guy just didn't show much interest in him. This was all very disappointing for

35

Joachim, who'd politely hoped to renew their friendship. Wearing a gaudy peach-colored Hawaiian shirt, Alfred introduced Joachim around. They were almost all university students, many of whom had come with their girlfriends. They looked around twenty-two, twenty-three years old. Perhaps because they were young, and because many of them already knew each other, their conversations rattled along, and I could barely understand a word. Occasionally I would make out a "cool," accompanied by a high-five, "stop it, please," "this is crazy, yeah?" all with a strong accent. Joachim went into the kitchen and came back with his paper plate loaded up with meat to cook on the electric hob, and cake spread with apricot jam. He explained to me that he didn't recognize many of the other guests because he'd only gone to school with them for a year. One girl, who arrived late and on her own, went around introducing herself to everyone as though she were the host. The majority of the girls wore skin-tight jeans and midriff-flashing T-shirts encrusted with fake gems or gold foil, cheap stuff they'd obviously bought at the discount store. Strangers mingled instantly, their eyes sparkling, starting up conversations even if they seemed to have nothing in common. However, were their companion to disappear, they never stood there hesitating or wandered awkwardly around the room, but straight away attached themselves to another group and launched into conversation. After hearing a few words of my faltering German they immediately realized what a miserable level my conversational skills were at, and would latch on to another, more exciting discussion as soon as the opportunity presented itself. They talked and talked incessantly, as though it would be a suffering akin to being buried alive for them to fall silent for even a moment, or simply for the stream of their words to slow down just a fraction. On and on, about something they'd seen on TV or something that had happened at school, relationships, the war that might break out in the future, going to study in America, employment, and so on. Fed up with trying and failing to force my way into a conversation, even though these weren't people I particularly wanted to spend time with, I got angry with Joachim. I didn't care if this was an authentic "student party," I wanted to go home. But at some point, Joachim came up behind me and said "If you pull a face like that, everyone here will think you're stuck up, full of yourself. And once they've decided that about you, that's it. This isn't Asia, alright? No one's going to show any interest in you if you just stand there all silent and moody. Just smile and join in, and if you listen hard enough one of these days you'll end up understanding what they're saying." He grinned broadly, remembering how things had been three years ago, when I'd had to make a big effort to understand his German. My progress then had all been down to M, but things were different now. I'd long since given up the idea of reaching such a level of fluency. It was simply that I couldn't stand the youths who had come to the party, either as individuals or as representatives of their whole clamorous, demanding society, whose sole virtue is its sociable affability. Smiling and greeting each other, shaking hands and exchanging superficial, perfunctory chatter, while knowing full well that such things are nothing but a waste of one's energies. I was angry with myself for being unable to explain all this to Joachim, to make him understand how I felt. All I could say was "I hate parties."

"Well, in that case you'll just have to go and sit with the smokers. But it might be pretty boring."

"I want to go home," I said in an undertone.

"What? You mean now? You must be joking. You're just being stuck up, and besides, people would be offended. I mean, it's just plain rude, helping yourself to food and drink then rushing off without even staying to celebrate, like your typical pauper."

"Typical pauper" was something I liked to call Joachim, and now here he was throwing it back at me.

"Who's there for me to celebrate with? The people who come to these parties transcend nationality, age, class, race; they're nothing but a bunch of uncultured idiots, damn it. Why should I put up with it?"

"Just hang on a bit longer, maybe you'll change your mind."

"I'm never coming to this kind of thing again. Why did you bring me?"

"Hey, you're the one who said you wanted to come! Don't be so neurotic." Joachim steered me into the kitchen, where he'd been chatting with some of the others. It was incredibly loud in there, the crowd of new arrivals getting food and opening beer bottles and greeting each other. Across the room I spotted a window seat that I hadn't noticed before, and wondered if I would be able to ensconce myself there without bothering with all the questions and handshakes and embraces. In order to reach that haven, though, I would have to make my way across the crowded kitchen, which seemed a veritable war zone to me. There was nothing I hated more than putting up with something when I wasn't in the mood, purely for the sake of social conventions—it was just too pointless. Just then, someone asked me for a cigarette. I said I didn't have any, adding that I didn't smoke. Right behind me, a group of students whom I'd met a long time ago were standing bunched together, talking all at once to each other about their grades and exams, complaining about their teachers and winter jobs. I couldn't be sure which of them had spoken to me. All I saw was an exceptionally large hand on the table.

"Really? What a shame. I mean, you used to enjoy having something in your mouth." Those last words were pronounced with particular relish. I turned to look behind me.

"Do I know you?" I addressed the first one my eyes landed upon—a short young man with exceptionally blue eyes shining in his darkly tanned face.

"Yeah. You came to Erich's party a few years ago. With M. Isn't that right? How's M doing? Haven't seen her for years." But he melted back into the group before I had the chance to reply, as if he'd never had any genuine interest in either me or M and had merely been mouthing empty formalities. My eyes picked out a familiar face from across the room—the guy who'd asked me for a cigarette. But I didn't recognize him. Joachim pushed his way through to me, holding my coat and his jacket. If you still want to go we can go now, he said. You want to go too? I asked, and Joachim replied I don't care, I really don't care.

"I can go on my own, Joachim. That way you'll be able to stay here as long as you want. It'll be fine, I'll get the subway from Friedrichstrasse then change at Alexanderplatz and get the tram."

"No, you can't. Do you even know how to get to Friedrichstrasse station from here? And if you change to get the tram it'll be a long walk from the subway station; you shouldn't do that alone, not at this time of night."

"Okay, in that case, let's both leave now." As soon as we put on our coat and jacket and made our way to the front door, the woman who had been introducing herself to everyone came up to us and smilingly asked Joachim where he was going.

"Are you leaving? Look, the fireworks are starting in twenty minutes; you don't want to miss that, do you? Then we'll open the wine and the party will really get going. Come on, stay and have some fun."

"Oh no, we're not leaving," Joachim said, "but she's got a bit of a headache." He indicated me. "We're just going to go downstairs and get some air."

"Oh? Well, come back soon, then, and I'll see you in a minute."

I said a curt goodbye to the woman, who was waving happily at me, and left, closing the door behind me. The blaring music was faintly audible even with the door closed. I went downstairs and, as I exited the building, saw fireworks explode in the distance. The gunpowder-scented air was cold, but wonderfully refreshing after the crowded rooms upstairs. I was glad I hadn't gritted my teeth and tried waiting it out. As we walked to the subway station the explosions grew progressively louder, coming thick and fast. Some were being let off near the entrance to the station, and even once we were safely underground the noise was really something. It was so loud it made my ears hurt.

"Did you tell Alfred you were leaving?" I asked Joachim, with my fingers stuck in my ears. He shook his head.

"Seemed better not to," he answered peevishly. "Just a bit longer and they would have opened the wine; it's all your fault."

"What? I told you I could go home on my own. You made the decision for yourself."

"You think anyone would want to talk to me with that haughty expression you had on? You looked so stuck-up."

"I didn't have a haughty expression."

"You just can't act like that at a party."

"I don't care about how you can and can't act at parties. And they were ignoring you too, Joachim. Like you didn't notice?"

"Most of them were just kids I went to gymnasium with, I don't know them that well. That's why. Anyway, I don't give a damn about that kind of thing either."

Joachim's friends had been to ordinary gymnasiums like him, and he'd wanted to show me that he was in with a certain crowd, the kind of crowd that included blonde Scandinavian girls. In those terms, his evening had been a failure; I guess that's just the way these things go. But his mention of the gymnasium reminded me of something.

"Joachim, one of them knew me from somewhere. Maybe he'd seen me at Erich's party, ages ago." Erich taught English at Humboldt gymnasium.

Joachim barely reacted, probably still thinking about the food, wine, and beer we'd left behind at the party. He was striding along with his arms crossed. It was now only ten minutes or so to midnight, when the fireworks would be let off in earnest. Walking the deserted streets at such an hour seemed like something only an idiot would do. Everyone else would have gathered together to celebrate, either in small groups of friends or at bigger, public parties, and those who preferred open spaces would brave the cold to go and watch the television broadcast being filmed at the Brandenburg Gate. Teenagers would be letting off fireworks in the small squares dotted here and there among the network of streets, and local kids would be lying in wait down dark alleys with firecrackers in their hands, waiting to let them off with a bang under the feet of passersby, then run away.

"So, how's M?" Joachim asked, as if the thought had suddenly struck him while we were waiting for the subway. "You must hear from her, right? She doing okay?" It was the first time he'd mentioned M.

"I'm not sure. We haven't met up or been in touch since the last time I was in Berlin."

Joachim was silent for a while, as if deep in thought. "Really?" he said eventually.

"I heard she was being treated by a French doctor who lives near Cité Foch. That's all."

"What do you mean, that's all? She's your oldest friend."

"She's the one who severed contact."

It was only two stops to Friedrichstrasse, so it wasn't too bad. The city center was thronged with people heading toward the Brandenburg Gate, kids planning to set off firecrackers on the subway, sour-faced policemen grumbling at having to work on New Year's Eve, and tourists wondering what was worth seeing. Joachim asked again if I wanted to go to the Brandenburg Gate, but I told him I didn't like that kind of thing.

"Just a little longer and they would have opened the wine," Joachim grumbled again. "It's all your fault."

We took the subway from Friedrichstrasse to Alexanderplatz, and from there had to physically shove our way through the surging tide of revelers in order to get to the tram stop. My jaw was tight with tension, conscious that a firework might explode next to me at any moment. Multicolored flowers of fire were blossoming in near-constant succession against the dark background of the sky. When we got onto the tram, Joachim looked at the clock and counted down to midnight.

"Three, two, one—now!"

We were sitting on the back seat in the last carriage, which was empty except for the two us, our bodies twisted round so that we could take in the scene outside through the window at the rear of the tram. Joachim did the countdown, and when the tram rounded the bend at Alexanderplatz the whole square was lit up by what seemed like a never-ending stream of fireworks, carving trails of cultured sparks across the sky. Three years earlier, M and I had gone to a fireworks display. But that had been an orderly, choreographed presentation, whereas New Year's Eve fireworks were an entirely different animal; something primitive, like a medieval hunt, or plague rampaging through a city, or a war in the barbarous Dark Ages. There were almost no other passengers on the tram. We turned to each other. *Frohes neues Jahr!* It was New Year's, after all.

"Just a bit longer and they would have opened the wine. Champagne, music, and we would have been celebrating New Year's at a party, where everything's warm and bright. Not some filthy, clapped-out tram. It's all your fault."

Joachim kept on muttering away to himself, like it was some tic he had. The tram pulled away from Alexanderplatz, and the fireworks followed us all the way to Mollstrasse and Hufelandstrasse, embroidering the sky like patterns on black silk. The numerous street parties had all reached their peak, and countless fireworks seemed to be being released simultaneously. Our tram was first attacked around Ernst-Thälmann-Park. Teenagers aimed their firecrackers at the wheels and windows of the tram, letting them off in a deafening cannonade. The whole city had become one big scintillating flash of light, lit by multicolored flares, and calling to mind images of Berlin during a bombing raid. Every time we turned a corner there were new gangs, their firecrackers already primed and ready, and the further we went into East Berlin the more serious it became. Not a single carriage got through unscathed, as long as there were passengers visible through the windows. Eventually, once we'd passed Thomas-Mann-Strasse and began heading in the direction of Ostsee, we ducked our heads beneath the glass window, hunching over like citizens of a bombed-out city cowering in an air-raid shelter. Joachim couldn't resist stressing his point one last time.

"This is all your fault."

Joachim had long maintained that, were he to become a successful entrepreneur, have a mansion built by the Spree and tear around in a sports car (though it was doubtful that a perfectly ordinary young engineer could ever amass such a fortune), the women whom his vast wealth would inevitably attract would be the icing on the cake, and he would have everything he could possibly desire. "Russian women, or Polish women, they're the best, because even the really pretty ones aren't fussy." His words dripped with contempt. And he wasn't joking; this was genuinely what he thought. "How on earth could anything be more important than money?" he said. "When it comes down to it, the reason you like M is that she's rich, isn't it? You're lying if you say otherwise." Joachim wasn't physically fragile like M, and he didn't suffer from allergies. He didn't drink alcohol and didn't smoke, though he would treat himself to the occasional joint if he happened to have a bit of spare money. He liked to affect a complete lack of interest in anything other than that which would be of some practical, tangible benefit or harm. He claimed that he wasn't afraid of dying, not in the least. According to him, what was there to be afraid of when it was just for the briefest of moments, and then the end? He claimed he would kill himself if he was unable to complete college, or some similar calamity befell him. He drew his index finger across his throat and made a short sharp sound, *kkik.* He would do it, he said, in the smoking room of the national library.

"*Kkik*, I'll make a quick end of it. Beats me why other people make such a big deal out of suicide. Those so-called 'artists' and 'intellectuals,' with their books and their plays and their essays. They're just trying to make a point with the kind of stuff they write about, being 'artistic' is just an excuse for them to kick up a fuss about something or other, something that'll get people talking. Money and fame, that's all anyone's after when it comes down to it."

While he was talking, Joachim poured a good slug of milk into his coffee and slathered a thick layer of jam over a slice of cake.

"Hmm, you must have read a lot about it to make a claim like that?"

"Oh yeah, they made us read all kinds of crap at school, really weird stuff, even though only some of it will come up in the *Abitur* and there's no way of telling what. For example, I had to read this one book called *The Tin Drum*, you know it? Insanely long, and even more tedious than Latin; the kind of thing where you don't have a clue what the hell it's supposed to mean even after you've read the whole thing. And it's all because of the language those writers use. They actually earn money for playing their clever little tricks! I mean, there's nothing wrong with plain German; there's no need to write books like that, the kind that make your mind go blank so you can't think of anything, or that use all these ambiguous words so it's so vague you can't be sure what any of it means. It's obviously all nonsense, just deliberately trying to confuse you. Beats me why I have to read those sorts of books if I want to become an engineer. I mean, just to put money in some writer's pocket? There's no other reason."

"You read Gunter Grass's *The Tin Drum*? You?"

"That's right. Can't you understand my German? I explained it as well as I could."

"I just wasn't expecting it, that's all. What do you remember from it?"

"I already told you! Not a single thing. I saw the film too; it was the worst damn film I ever saw. But weirdly enough, it's popular—really popular. That guy must be absolutely rolling in it. And that means he must have plenty of women hanging off him, too."

"Stop talking like an idiot, Joachim."

"What's idiotic about it? You and M like each other because you're both rich, no? Do you suppose there's some other reason?"

During the time he spent in civilian service, which he did instead of military service, Joachim had been assigned to a geriatric hospital attached to an old people's home. Naturally this wasn't a position he'd applied for, but once he'd been assigned the post there was no getting out of it. Ideally, the job required someone with a certain amount of tact and empathy, and Joachim by his own admission was far from sensitive. Neither did he hold all that much respect for those who were. All the same, he'd barely ever spoken about his experiences working there. For a young man just past twenty, the memories of that time were not especially pleasant.

"It was where the hospital sent all the serious cases—well, no, not serious cases, I mean, it wasn't like they were critically ill or anything, just that the doctors had decided it was no use treating them any more. They were just too old, so whatever illness they had, or else the treatment they'd had for it, had left them so weak and feeble they were incapacitated. Or, you know, there were the ones who didn't particularly need to be in a hospital. Anyway, once they came to this place, that was it for them. They would just lie in their beds, waiting to die. Not that anyone thought this was some kind of tragedy, I mean, they were old, it was natural. Every night the old women would crap themselves and in the mornings I had to wash all their underwear. Can you imagine what that was like? Not just what it felt like to have to do it, but what it actually looked like, and the smell. We had to wash them by hand, not just give them a once-over with the showerhead; they insisted that was the only way to get them properly clean. I never understood why we couldn't just use the toilet brushes. And how those old women came to have such enormous genitals, that's something else I never got my head around. These huge things, all wrinkled and withered; dry as a bone no matter how often you washed them. I'm not lying, their underwear was like a giant's black galoshes. And they were almost all women, you know. Maybe because women tend to live longer. Can you imagine how agonizing it was for them, the ones who weren't lucky enough to have a quick end? It was more than just physical pain. I mean, who wouldn't be in agony, having to live like that? But it wasn't just that they were so immobile they were more like just bodies than actual people, it was that there was nothing they could do themselves; they had no opportunity to make their own decisions. They couldn't even choose to die on their own, someone would have to help them. But it doesn't have to be like that—all it takes is a quick *kkik* at the decisive moment, and it's all over. Simple as that. Meanwhile we civvies joke about how we can't wait to get out of there, but as long as those disgusting places keep being built they'll keep on sending new invalids there to die. Of course, there's plenty of kids in this country that have to do that kind of work, but when you're young—ugh, it's enough to make you sick."

Gulping down a mouthful of coffee and flicking through yesterday's *Tagesspiegel*, he added: "You're going to die like that too, you know. It's just a matter of time."

"What makes you think that?"

"Because there isn't any other option. Don't you think?"

"Well, what's your secret, then?"

"I'm not going to end up like that. Men don't, generally speaking. And I'm not going to live that long anyway. Seriously, if someone promised me a really long life, I'd tell them thanks, but no thanks. No clinging on to life for me, I'm going to go quickly. And I'm not scared of dying, not in the least—I know it's strange, but it's the truth."

Mental shallowness, poverty of thought, is no different from death. That was M's belief. That a mind deficient in serious thought is no better than a lump of rotting meat. Even though we consider death to be a concrete, physical, temporally bounded phenomenon, the compass of our lives can be comprehended in the abstract concept of death ahead of this end point. In other words, there are those of us who are already dying from the moment they are born. In M's opinion, Joachim was one such individual. And so when he boasts about how he's not afraid of dying, trotting it out like a stock phrase, when he claims that the prospect of death—in other words, the prospect of his mind no longer being conscious—holds absolutely no dread or anxiety for him, this is no lie. At first, when I didn't know M very well, I naturally found this judgment extremely harsh. But after I came to know her better, I realized that M's idea of humanity transcends any sense of personal intimacy or human affection, that for M it is a concept that exists outside of the human race. M was coldly, sometimes cruelly precise when it came to assessing Joachim, but this was never a personal attack. Rather than simply being critical of Joachim as an individual, her appraisal was in fact based upon a pessimistic indictment of humanity as a whole. Joachim was perfectly aware of all this, but it didn't bother him. On the contrary, he would confront M with the opposite argument. He would ask, grandly and loudly, since it was clear that not everybody shared M's artistic inclinations, for what reason, then, did everyone have to be absorbed in an abstract world, and think that nothing outside that world could be beautiful, and look down their noses at television, which provided an inexpensive source of relaxation? M had always been contemptuous of Joachim's limited analytical capabilities and narrow-minded opinions, and he would always turn this around and accuse her criticisms of being derivative. And so, listening to their debate, if such a thing could be called a debate, Joachim couldn't help but appear more and more idiotic and obstinate. He was hardly au fait with intellectual discussions, and certainly found no enjoyment in them. But, thinking about it now with the benefit of hindsight, I would hazard that rather than being genuinely unable to follow M's train of thought, it was simply that he couldn't agree with her reasoning. Plus, his ability to logically argue for a point that he himself did not agree with was sorely limited. He didn't know how to talk in terms of abstract concepts or general postulates. And so the only option left open to him was to continuously deny the validity of the other person's point.

At that time, M was living near the Winter Park. On days when we didn't have a class with her, Joachim and I would visit her on our way home from the library. I don't know how that park came to be called the Winter Park. After all, it existed in other seasons too, not just winter. But the green iron signboard at its entrance declared it to be "Winter Park, Hohenschönhausen." After a heavy snowfall, children flocked there with their sleds, which they would haul up to the park's hilly areas. The biggest thrill was to be had in riding them down the frozen, sloping footpaths. In winter, stark, bare deciduous trees and small green firs were mantled in snow, frozen hard like biscuits left in the refrigerator. M's house was on the edge of a thickly wooded street at the rear of the park. Because of the shade from the trees, the houses there got very little light and so it always felt colder there than elsewhere. Instead of catching a bus from the nearby tram stop where we got off, it was much quicker for Joachim and I to walk to M's through the woods. The snow lying unmelted on the trails had been there for some time. In fact, several weeks had passed since it fell, but even though it had long since vanished from the roads and the rooftops, in the constant shade of the trees it lay glittering cold and magnificent, as if it had fallen only the night before. Entering into the very heart of the woods, where even the rattle of the tram was no longer audible, we would find ourselves in an ice-bound kingdom of wintry silence. The woods seemed as though they'd been locked in eternal winter by some enchantment, until the housing complexes at the rear of the park came into view around a corner. I once saw a huge snowman standing there. At least a week had passed since the snow had fallen, but the snowman was still almost completely intact, an open black umbrella stuck upright into the crown of its head, a crumpled page from a film program lying at its feet. Visible through the trees, the sky was overcast as though with the smoke from something burning. But as the sun sank below the horizon, a faint, honeyed light briefly draped the western sky. The world of the woods was washed with the colors of winter and evening and the setting sun. Then the snow began to fall, wet and cold on cheeks, lips, and hair. All of a sudden we found we had left the heart of the woods, which had seemed like another world, behind. The entrance to the housing complex at the rear of the park came back into view. M's apartment was on the very edge of the complex. We rang the bell at the front entrance, hurried inside when the door was buzzed open, and went up to M's apartment on the fourth floor. Inside the centrally heated building, sensation rapidly returned to our numbed extremities. Our cheeks flushed red and our heads thrummed gently, as if we'd each inhaled a lungful of cigarette smoke. Joachim always ran up the stairs three or four paces ahead of me, impatient to get inside the warm room as soon as possible and thaw his body with a cup of coffee. He greeted M noncommittally on entering and, without removing his shoes, went to nose around the kitchen, even examining the contents of the fridge. After running his fingers over her computer, opening the lid of the piano and tinkling the keys, changing the television channel, eating some of the cookies and chocolate that were laid out on the coffee table, and pouring himself a cup of coffee from the thermos, he eventually stretched out on the sofa to flick through a magazine. Once, he managed to complete this sequence while I was still laboring up the stairs, and I found him already lying on the sofa chewing the last of the cookies when I walked in. M held the door open for me after Joachim came in. Her apartment generally tended to be darker than his. Or rather, this darkness was unalleviated by any electric lighting. And so, panting my way up the stairs and entering the old apartment through the half-open door, I would come face to face with that darkness, which always gave off a peculiar smell, light and sweet, like a dried orange just beginning to rot. It was of the same intensity as the shadows that envelop a place from which the sun has withdrawn completely, akin to that realm encountered in dreams, the utter black directly before surfacing from sleep. Even when I didn't know M all that well, that darkness made a very great impression on me. Once I'd stood in front of the door for a short while, objects slowly began to take on solid forms. The faintest of lights seeped into the apartment from who knew where, kindling the silent, solitary existence of inanimate objects, gifting them with the palest hues, whispered words, the barest outlines of physical form. Bare green walls; a narrow corridor covered with a small, worn rug; the door of a wall cupboard where umbrellas and shoes were stored; the faint scent of furniture polish; two rooms with bare wooden floors, their doors lying half-open; a low voice coming from behind that door; the sound of someone leafing through a book. And I enter the apartment and close the door.

After some time had passed, I discovered the following passage in a book I was reading:

> Early one evening, we arrived at a village of mud huts.
> The huts were an unsightly pale brown, and stood in
> stark relief against the vast and otherwise empty plain.

A railroad cut across the plains from the west. We came out from there and had to stand in two lines along the rail tracks.

I never saw such a desolate place. There was simply nothing, in all directions, as far as the eye could see. The only thing to attract the eye was the far horizon disappearing in a faint light. There was nothing but dust, dust everywhere. It was dreary beyond belief.

A Chinese prisoner whispered to me that this area was the start of a place known as "Shinjang"; some truly dire things were rumored about it. He said that we would now be hauled through the Lop Nur desert, where the Chinese government had apparently tested nuclear weapons; up until the Turpan reservoir it was nothing but a city of convicts. In other words, thousands of people incarcerated in hundreds of POW camps.

I had no idea why that passage made me think of M and the period at the beginning of our acquaintance when I'd been a regular visitor at her apartment. M wasn't Chinese, after all, and as far as I could recall we'd never discussed either China or prisons. There's absolutely nothing to attract the eye in this place, it's the kind of place where the only view is of the desolate desert and the far horizon clustered with dust clouds, and all that is now left for me is to pass the remainder of my days as one among thousands of nameless prisoners, in the filthy, wretched POW camp. I couldn't grasp why such a terrible plight would make me think of M and those visits. But as I read the passage I was transported, finding myself directly in front of the door to M's apartment, at the rear of the Winter Park, staring at the darkness inside. When you encounter a situation in which there is absolutely no opportunity for making any decision; when your immediate environment is unremittingly desolate, lacking even the means for you to distinguish directions; when you're imprisoned as a nameless number, when your individuality is nullified and you become merely one among many—even if you call it by a very different name, even if they aren't quite identical, such an experience is, at the very least, closely akin to death.

After the New Year's Eve party and the New Year's music concert, Joachim left for Schleswig-Holstein. He told me that the meister to whom he'd been apprenticed when he first learned to weld had a job which needed finishing over the year-end holiday, and had offered to pay Joachim to come and help out, along with room and board at his workshop in Flensburg. Until the last week in January, when Joachim had to come back in order to sit the end of term exams, I would stay by myself in his apartment and look after his dog Benny. It snowed or rained every couple of days, and the trams went past at seven- or twenty-minute intervals. In the mornings, before the day dissolved the darkness, the sound of Benny padding about woke me from my sleep. Benny waited patiently by the kitchen door while I made coffee and ate bread and honey. But when I'd put on my jacket and boots and attached the lead to Benny's collar, he would make an agonized sound as if swallowing a sob. He must have been pining for Joachim. On days when it wasn't snowing I took Benny for a walk as far as the cemetery, where dogs and bicycles were forbidden. While I strolled around among the gravestones, Benny waited at the bicycle stand, seemingly expecting either Joachim or I to appear at any moment. If the front doorbell rang or footsteps could be heard outside, Benny's ears instantly pricked up. But he would quickly realize that it wasn't Joachim. Stricken with grief, the dog slept on Joachim's

53

slippers. He stared constantly at the table on which Joachim had left his book of general physics theory. I held Benny the way Joachim had and spoke to him in a muffled voice, my face buried in the scruff of his neck. My love, my love, my only one, stay. I'll be right back. Good boy, my love.

5) When the weather improved a little in the second week of January, I ventured out a couple of times in search of a café, one that had a breakfast menu and was suitably near to Joachim's apartment. The one I discovered was ten minutes away by tram, so not exactly in the immediate area, but a walk of that length was no inconvenience. I'd actually stumbled upon it quite by chance, while taking Benny for a walk. It wasn't expensive, and the frothy café au lait was really good. The café was fairly small, and hidden away on a corner at the end of a craftsman's street rather than being out on the main road where the tram passed by, but plenty of people sought it out. It was impossible to find an empty seat at weekends, but on a weekday afternoon the roomy window seat was almost always free, and I could take my time buttering my bread and drinking my coffee while reading which-ever book I'd brought. And dogs were allowed inside, so it was good for Benny too. The café even had a set menu for dogs, but I only bought it for Benny every other time. Joachim hadn't men-tioned anything about the café even though, having lived in this area for several years, there was no way he wouldn't know about it. On weekday mornings he usually took the tram and subway as far as Danziger Strasse to have breakfast. I wasn't fond of Danziger Strasse. The street itself was wide but felt chaotic and disorganized. They'd widened the street with the original intention of putting up some fine buildings, but for some reason this plan had been almost

immediately abandoned, and so all that remained were shabby second-hand clothes stores and cluttered tattoo studios, the pavement was narrow and uneven, and the jarring contrast of the road's incredible width made the place seem as though it was falling apart. It was a place littered with ugly, hastily erected buildings, a vast place, where dust motes from the countryside danced in the bus station. But it was also the location of Joachim's favorite breakfast café; at weekends they served a buffet, it was cheap, it was tasty, and there were lots of dishes to choose from. The downside was that if you went early in the morning there was no way you'd get a seat. I brought Joachim's copy of *American Psycho* to breakfast there one morning, purely for the sake of having something to read, but in the end I couldn't get on with it. There was nothing in the book to justify my initial interest in it. It was the same with the books on physics and art, and the *Harry Potter* series. Personally, I really liked the Baedeker travel books; compared with other travel books, which tend to rely too heavily on photographs, they allow a relatively large amount of space for description, prose essays, historical background, literary quotations or reproductions of artworks, that kind of thing. In spite of the practical information which they also contained, the Baedekers provided more pleasure and fulfillment than many other books, the kind that are light on intelligence and stuffed full with hyperbole. But unfortunately Joachim's Baedekers were all ones I also owned, or else had previously read somewhere. I wanted to read something properly, not just in order to pass the time at the café, so I relaxed my budget and went to a bookshop in the city center. There, I chose three books. The first was Kafka's *The Castle*; I've no idea why I chose it. Not only had I already read it a long time ago, but I hadn't even found it all that interesting when I did. Perhaps I bought it because when I discovered it in the bookshop it made me remember the

Max Anderson comics I'd read the last time I was in Berlin. I hadn't been studying German for very long when I read them; there was a scene where the heroine, Akina, gets a call in the middle of the night demanding that she reads *The Castle*. She has to stay up all night to finish it, and after that she's told she has to read *Crime and Punishment*. But for some reason or other I couldn't concentrate on *The Castle*. I think at first I'd been a bit daunted, but contrary to my preconceptions it wasn't particularly difficult, in fact I was quite surprised by how simple some of the sentences seemed. But that didn't help me focus on it. I was determined to read it the whole way through, but in the end I found I couldn't manage it so I left it at Joachim's house, along with a brief note saying that I hoped he would read it; he didn't, of course. The two other books I bought were *People Who Read Books* and *Forms of Human Coexistence*. I read them when I'd begun to tire of my usual routine of eating breakfast at the café, taking the tram to the park, being unable to sleep at night, watching television, listening to music etc. Of course, I wasn't reading them very carefully, and I set them aside whenever turning the pages became too much of an effort. Later, I occasionally bumped into people who had read *People Who Read Books*; naturally, when I said I liked reading, they were quick to recommend it to me. Some of them were able to appreciate good writing, but not the majority, and in fact many of them had a taste in books that I would have scorned. I guessed that the reason they liked it was because of the closing section, which became sentimental as it aspired to tragedy. It had been a bestseller here, in the positive sense of the word. The writing certainly had a way of pulling you in. One day, when I'd just recently started the book, I took the tram late at night. I'd gone out late in the afternoon with no particular destination in mind, eaten Thai soup at a standing bar, listened to music at a late-opening vinyl record store on Friederichstrasse, chosen a book at the bookshop, and was on my way home. I found an unoccupied seat on the tram, sat down, and opened *People Who Read Books*. It was very dark outside the window, so there was nothing to distract my concentration. I read on. Beautiful, arrestingly unfamiliar sentences appeared in front of me, vanishing into the darkness outside the window. Beautiful and complex, they frequently included words that were relatively new to me. I concentrated on each sentence one by one, and had to read them several times in order to understand how the many subclauses related to each other, using the context to try and work out the meaning of certain words. The further I pushed my way through the thorny thicket of the sentences, the more I faltered, and even found that I'd unwittingly been sounding out the words as I read them. I wanted to hear the music of the writing, just as M had in the old days. Joachim was the one who'd introduced us. I'd already been taking lessons from a German language tutor, alongside a Vietnamese girl whose vocabulary vastly outstripped mine, as she'd lived in Switzerland for several years. On top of that, our lessons were structured around the university entrance exam for foreigners that the Vietnamese girl was planning to take. I couldn't care less about the university entrance exam and hated that kind of lesson, so I'd been thinking about taking a short private course, even though I couldn't really afford it. But it was incredibly difficult to find a suitable private tutor, as private tutoring wasn't common in Germany. Joachim had sounded fairly diffident when he first mentioned M, stressing that he wasn't sure what she'd be like as she wasn't a vocational teacher. According to him, M was a student at the language school and (this was his expression) absolutely off her head about music; the two of them had taken a maths course together. He left me in front of M's house and headed off to school. At out first meeting I could barely understand her, confused both by her unfamiliar pronunciation and (to me) convoluted way of expressing herself. She was tall and androgynous, even beautiful, but seemed as though she would be strict. Before I had time to amend that first impression, and without so much as greeting me, M handed me a book and told me to read it out loud, adding that I should take care to pronounce the words properly whether or not I understood them. I glanced at the title but couldn't make any sense of it, and when I opened the book and began haltingly to read, the passage I'd landed on proved equally incomprehensible. It's a shame, but I can't even remember what that book was, now— the first book in German I ever read, aside from a grammar text-book. My pronunciation was, of course, atrocious; I stuttered and often misread the words, couldn't tell where I should pause and where I had to keep going, couldn't get a feel for the rhythm, and mangled everything with my foreign accent. I can assert with complete confidence that M did not understand a word I read that day. It was our first lesson.

Our subsequent lessons continued with the same format, of me reading aloud things I couldn't understand and M trying to piece together the actual substance of the passages, the expression on her face constantly changing, shading into sadness, suffering, surprise, tedium, wistfulness, expressionlessness, defiance, rejection, desire. Once in a while M would ask me to repeat a certain passage. And so I read it again, still without understanding, struggling to pronounce the words clearly. What is this? I trembled with anger and need as I sat in front of M, unable to make any sort of emotional connection with what I was reading. The difference between understanding and not understanding was all too conclusive, like that between a rich man and a poor man, so I didn't dare ask any questions for fear of revealing my ignorance. *People Who Read Books* makes me think of that time. The people I met and talked with about books (in Germany, anyway) had all read *People Who Read Books*, so naturally M also had a copy; it's possible that it was one of the various books I read sections from during our lessons. Of course this is just conjecture, not something I really remember. After I'd read a page, M would choose a particular word or sentence and launch into a lengthy explanation. One example was for the word "desolate." "Do you know what 'desolate' means? You don't? Of course, one could simply say, 'when there is nothing visually arresting,' but that would only be a very irresponsible and conventional definition. Something can be desolate irrespective of its visual appearance. The meaning is a little different. For example, when everything is all the same color, like a desert, and there are many buildings but they are inhabited only by scorpions, everyone has left, there are no wells anywhere, or the train station is too far away. The nuance is a little different from when something is tedious or insipid. So why do we say 'desolate'? Rather than 'bleak' or 'empty,' that is. Can you talk a little about how you would use those words in a sentence? And give some examples of the different impressions which they give, to explain how they compare?" I was unable to muster a response. Having barely mastered the rudiments of the German language, M's first lesson was so far above my level it was almost cruel. Blushing furiously, instead of thinking about how to answer M's question I made up my mind there and then to ask Joachim to find me a different German tutor, one who was a little more good-natured and accustomed to foreigners. But in the end, I never did.

I would read a certain sentence, go to turn the page then, hesitating, read the sentence again. "Would you please repeat that last sentence one more time," M often asked me, "the one you just read." M listened so intently it was as though she was breathing the sentence in, appropriating it for herself, whereas to me it was nothing but a meaningless string of syllables. Jerked back to reality, I opened my eyes and saw that I was the only passenger on the tram, which had now stopped. Glancing down at the book in my hand, I saw that I'd only read three pages, but I seemed to have been lost in my memories for an awfully long time. The tram remained stationary for too long for it to have merely stopped at a red signal or to be changing drivers. The carriage I was in still had its lights on, but outside the window the darkness was impenetrable. Rain was trickling down the tram's windows. Intent on my book, I'd missed the announcement for my station and had come right to the end of the line, to a place called Ahrensfelde, on the very edge of Berlin. I'd never been there before. The tram was sitting there with its doors open, and when I stepped down from the carriage I could just about make out some low hills in the distance, but there were no buildings, no lights, not even any streetlamps. I turned to look back at the tram, stopped there in the middle of the track with the rain coming down. The driver had already left. There were no bus stops, no passersby, no shops or phone booths. With darkness rendering the landscape featureless, it occurred to me that I could well be standing in the middle of a vast steppe, the haunt of prowling wolves. On top of all this, the falling rain was icy cold. I wasn't sure of the time, and could only hazard a guess that it was still a little before midnight. Already soaked through, I followed the tracks back up in the direction the tram had come from, convinced that there had to be a bus stop somewhere. Silence, cold, darkness, no traces of human life—if such things are what's commonly called desolate, then this place was desolate. Conventionally, the word may be more often used to describe a desert or wasteland of some kind, but it can equally apply to a bare, lonely railroad station that you've only come to by mistake, where there are no buildings and no signs of life. To be honest, though, it's difficult for me to distinguish between "desolate," "bare," "lonely," "abandoned," "empty," which all seem to mean something quite similar. My understanding of their various nuances is sketchy, to say the least. What M tried to teach me wasn't so much the meaning of each individual word, but the absolute, universal concepts to which the words referred, those fundamental concepts which each of the many languages in this world calls by a different name. Such concepts do not recognize national borders, do not make up a sovereign state, and are all equally close to the center they cluster around. Also, since each word has a wide spectrum of possible meanings, it has to be read within the specific context of each given appearance. Using verbose, unwieldy expressions where several simple ones would do can come across as pretty boorish; in fact, M liked to refer to it as "barbarian." Ultimately, "learning a foreign language" is too simplistic an expression for a process which is more like crossing a border; similarly, an individual's development as a human being is only possible through language, not because language is our only means of communication, but because it is the only tool precisely calibrated for the application of critical thought. But to me, these thoughts of M's were nothing but phantoms. A mother tongue isn't a border that can just be crossed, not even with the strongest will in the world. Even after fully mastering a foreign language (if such a thing is ever possible), your mother tongue still acts as a prison for your consciousness—this wasn't a view that M ever expressed in so many words, but I knew that it was true. The fact that my mother tongue was different from M's caused me unbearable grief.

After I'd walked a little way I came across another tram, also stopped in the middle of the tracks with its lights on. The doors of the first carriage were open, and the driver—I could tell that was who she was by the uniform she was wearing—was leaning against

the door, reading a book. I went up to her and asked where I could
catch a tram going back into the city, and she pointed across the
road to a bus stop and platform that I hadn't noticed before. As
if to make up for the general desolation of the place, these were
glittering like a phantasm, like a cloud of glowing insects suddenly
birthed from the nighttime fields. The platform clock showed
11.45. The driver told me that if I waited here for five minutes,
a tram would arrive that would then head back the other way. As
luck would have it, it was a Saturday, when the trams run all night.
I waited on the wet platform, and sure enough a tram pulled in
before long. After the new driver got in, they switched direction
at the end of the tracks and drove back they way they'd come. The
driver who'd been reading a book must have finished her run ahead
of schedule and been waiting to clock off. When the tram I was on
pulled away from the platform she was still reading, leaning against
the door of the other, empty tram, which shone like a beacon amid
the dark fields. There was no one else on the platform. I found my
place in my book, and sat down again.

Forms of Human Coexistence was by a young writer from Leipzig,
about his experiences living in America. The writer's father was
the playwright and novelist Christoph Hein; I remembered having
heard his name before. I chose the book because it was printed
clearly in a large typeface, and had photographs which broke up
the monotony of the prose (something that usually irritates me
when I'm reading in Korean, but with German it was helpful to
have a break now and again); it caught my attention because I'd
recently become interested in works by young East German writers. The fact that it was about America was neither here nor there
for me. The book clearly didn't set out to be taken seriously, yet, as
I read it, I often found myself unable to suspend a properly critical
judgment, and every now and then I'd come across a part which I

found unconvincing. The writer had spent his teenage years long-
ing for New York, which to him was all street gangs and gunfights
and stylish, sexy women who hail taxis to shuttle between bars
and breakdancing classes. Back then, though, it wasn't easy for an
East German to get permission to travel abroad; you almost always
had to wait until you were an old-age pensioner, sixty-five years
old at least. All the same, he never abandoned his dream. In the
end he managed to find a way around the various obstacles that
lay in his path, though some of this was more through luck than
initiative, and traveled to America as soon as he finished school
at eighteen. Whenever I picked up the book I would open it at
random and begin to read from there, and as I didn't mark off
the pages I'd already read I frequently ended up rereading certain
parts. I couldn't ever be sure whether I'd read the whole thing or
not, especially as there'd been certain especially difficult sections
that I'd had to abandon. I found the opening section incredibly

63

disappointing, especially considering that the author was a young
East German, stuffed as it was with adolescent hankerings after an
idealized New York. All the same, I didn't set the book aside. His
writing fairly zipped along, enlivened by a jaunty tone and a wit
that could be incredibly cutting. He clearly enjoyed showcasing his
literary talents, and if all this wasn't quite as effortless as he made it
seem, the effect at least was there. I was so fucking happy, making
out like nothing bothered me; his writing was littered with expressions like these. On the one hand, this was no doubt an accurate
rendering of an eighteen-year-old's feelings on visiting America for
the first time, but it was equally clear that it was a pose, carefully
calculated to give the reader a very specific impression of who the
writer was. In any case, it was the wittiest book I'd ever read—or at
least, that I could remember having read—with the possible exception of some by Milan Kundera. According to an online review,

which I looked up on one of the bookshop's computers, his writing possessed a "merciless wit that is at the same time completely fresh and unaffected"; I didn't think that was an exaggeration. But this was more than just a sharp wit occasionally deployed. His words were like scurrying rats, constantly seeking for something to sink their teeth into. He was also perfectly aware of the effect of his descriptions, which seemed to revel in a particularly cruel strain of mockery. Overall, he was unsentimental, and his descriptions of his travels demonstrated a total lack of awareness of even the possibility that such things might benefit from a deeper, more nuanced treatment, however vague the intellectual framework, or that he might more profitably have employed a more macroscopic point of view now and then, zooming out from the minutiae in order to get a sense of the bigger picture, but he was also hell-bent on hunting down individual subjects upon which to deploy his

eviscerating sarcasm without any slackening of the tempo, like a child of badly-off parents who has finally gotten his hands on an expensive toy to satiate that all-consuming greed which people call curiosity (probably for the simple reason that he was East German, he seemed extremely wary that his writing not be saddled with that already hackneyed label, "East German melancholy"); for all of these reasons I was initially impatient, wishing that he would take a break from his outsider's-perspective depiction of the lives of the urban American underclass. Given that such scenes hardly represented anything new for those familiar with big cities, that there was nothing novel or unique about them, at first I'd questioned whether it was really necessary to write such a book; needlessly, as it turned out, because in the end I was convinced that the author's decision had been the right one. The narrative sped along, relentlessly satirizing those representatives of the urban poor with whom the author came into contact (some of whom could even be described as lacking a moral compass), poking its tongue out at the reader now and then, and far too taken up with all this to leave room for any serious considerations; compared with its incisive yet light-hearted style, the weight and import of the writing were absurdly one-dimensional—trivial fluff, really—meaning the writer couldn't help but come across as little more than a young man caught up in his own caprices, admittedly with some literary talent, but only of an ordinary, trifling kind. As I said, this was my initial opinion, which underwent a radical turnaround as I read more of the book—so radical, in fact, as to leave me a little suspicious. Later, though, it occurred to me that had the writer adopted a position of serious social commentary, I might well have simply stereotyped his writing as yet another example of "East German melancholy," just what readers like me would unconsciously be predisposed to expect given his age and nationality. Each page had a color picture, pop-art style, and perhaps it was impossible not to dismiss what the writer was doing as merely taking a dig at everything, with the unbounded confidence in his own project common to those who have grown up having praise heaped upon their slightest achievement. It was even possible that its light-hearted tone came off badly because I read it straight after *People Who Read Books*. After all, Jakob Hein was only eighteen when he left for America, and the book remained faithful to the emotions that had moved him at the time. Rather than an objective look back at youth from the distant vantage point of adulthood, *People Who Read Books* is a paean to a boyhood love. As time passed I became increasingly eager to read Hein's debut, *My First T-Shirt*; there was clearly something in his bold, audacious attitude that made people want to return to his work, though I still can't quite put my finger on it. If I'd had time for another quick trip to the bookshop before I left then I might have been able to pick up a copy, but unfortunately it wasn't to be. Were the opportunity to arise in the future, I would make sure to slough off any traces of the critic, who holds certain preconceptions about the "lives of the East German *Jugend*" (something I was already sick of hearing about), and who has their scathing attitude honed and ready even before embarking upon the first page; what's more, I felt sure that I would be able to do so quite easily, even with pleasure.

During that period I had no phone and no Internet, though it would have been easy enough to track down an Internet café if I'd wanted to. The only things that marked the passage of time in any regular way were my thrice-daily walks with Benny. At first these were purely for Benny's sake, but they gradually came to be important for me, too. One at half past seven in the morning, one between two and three in the afternoon, and one which varied slightly, but was generally around nine in the evening. Twice a week I took an extra walk to the café for their set breakfast, sometime in between the usual morning and afternoon walks. At half past seven on a winter's morning, the sky was only just starting to lighten in the east, over Poland, and the darkness still lingered over the earth. I really hated having to get out of bed at that hour, when I awoke to bitter cold and it was still dark outside the window. But Benny was waiting. Whenever Joachim had to go to work or school he would take Benny for a walk beforehand, at six thirty. Since Benny was used to relieving himself at that hour, I couldn't put it off until later. Once outside, walking among the bare, white birches in the park and watching the sun come up, my dislike of the early hour vanished. The morning walk was usually a short one, only ten or fifteen minutes, but the post-lunch walk was longer, as long as there was no rain or snow. As the days started to warm up a little I began listening to music while I walked. I only had one CD with me, so I ended up listening to the same thing over and over again. On those extremely rare winter days when the sun was shining, even if it was only a faint gleam, it felt like the most wonderful gift anyone could possibly have given me. Besides, Benny always had plenty of energy in the afternoons, so we would give our legs a good stretch and often ended up going quite a long way. I used to have a detailed map of the city, when I was here three years ago, which had come in handy whenever I'd had to track down a post office, or the customs house, or the zoo, etc. But it had disappeared; I must have lost it somewhere. If I'd still had it I would have been able to study the roads and alleyways, and search for any castles or churches that might be worth going to have a look at, any small parks or dog cemeteries. I should have picked up a map when I went into the city center to buy a book. But I hadn't, because I hadn't been planning to go out much aside from the necessary walks, and I'd thought that having a map would render the streets overly familiar, stripping them of some of their allure. Around this time, I started to have a recurring nightmare; it begins with my accidentally bumping into someone I know. I'm at the café or the theater or the amusement park, or on the tram. Somewhere full of people. And someone comes up and speaks to me. Wow, it's been a long time. How are you doing these days? Where do you live now? And in the end, of course, the inevitable question: How's M? It's been ages since I saw her. These people have no clear identity, I'm just vaguely aware that I know them from somewhere. Finally, unsettled and even frightened, I open my eyes. No one has hurt me, no one has threatened me or forced me to do anything. They'd just happened to spot me as they were walking alone, came up to speak to me, and then disappeared. All perfectly natural. They all run through the same sequence, in exactly the same way. And then they go away, without bothering to wait for my answer. Even as the dream unfolds I know exactly how it's going to turn out, the same way it always does, but it's still such a relief when I wake up, and think to myself how lucky I am that it was only a dream.

Music was my other great love aside from reading, and the reason I made such an effort to stick to a strict budget. If money had been no object, I would have bought new CDs every week. Joachim didn't have a stereo, only the kitchen radio, but he'd borrowed some computer speakers from a college friend for me to hook up to a handheld CD player. CDs were expensive, so I liked to go the store on Friedrichstrasse and use their listening station, but since there were always other people waiting to use it you couldn't really listen to anything for very long. Plus, you had to stand up the whole time. Of course, you could always go up to the second floor, wait in line at the customer service center, hand over your ID so they would let you borrow one of their CD players, for in-store use only, take it downstairs to the classical music corner and listen to whatever you liked for as long as you liked, in one of their comfortable chairs. While I was saving up, I listened over and over again to one of the few CDs I already owned, Kim Kashkashian performing Shostakovich's Sonata for Violin and Piano. And so, on the night I'm remembering, the last night of the blizzard that year, with the road to the cemetery completely blanketed in snow and thus indistinguishable from its surroundings, with Joachim's bicycle no more than a smooth white mound, and the light from the lamp lost in the swirling snow, with the chill leaching in through the windowpane, I cracked *Forms of Human Coexistence* open and laid it on the kitchen table, put my feet up on a chair (I was wearing two pairs of thick woolen socks), and listened to Shostakovich's final sonata. I became Jakob Hein from

Leipzig, "coexisting with humans" in a state of great perplexity, experiencing all the inconveniences of linguistic communication on the crowded, diverse New York streets—he recounted how he'd assumed he'd be able to get by perfectly well with his English skills, but in New York the first person who'd been more or less able to understand him was a Korean taxi driver who'd only been living there for two months. There was nothing in the book that struck me as unusual—New Yorkers seem to be incapable of being surprised by anything any more, and consider nothing strange these days—and so, even though it wasn't as though I was hankering for something less familiar or more surprising, and in spite of its short, light-hearted essays, I was bored. I only managed a single sentence before I turned to gaze out of the window, listening to the music with my chin in my hand, threw away the cold dregs of the coffee, made some more, rummaged around in the fridge but found nothing new then, after one more sentence, gazed out of the window again. And then, finally, the third movement began.

6) Erich was my third German teacher; he also ended up being my last. The lessons with M only continued for a month, as by the end of this time we were living together and our relationship was no longer that of teacher and pupil. We had many conversations, but these weren't lessons. We both agreed that I needed a different German teacher; that M and I had, by this point, grown too close for her to fulfill this role. Besides, M's method of teaching left me floundering, out of my depth, yet she refused to teach "as if instructing children at grammar school." For M, literature was the highest and yet most fundamental use of language, meaning she believed in starting her pupils on literature and only later "demoting" them to grammar. She was so secure in

this belief that there was no room for any objection. Extremely unhappy, I refused to read the linguistics book she recommended, but at the same time was forever getting myself worked up over not knowing the precise way to use separable verbs and reflexive verbs. Picking up on the fact that my German still hadn't improved much beyond "serviceable," Joachim insisted that I make M return the lesson fees. He couldn't understand how on the one hand I was using predicates meaning "solid depiction of conditions" and "establishment of description," or (to him) senseless expressions like "hybridity of words," and asking him to explain absurd phrases which no one used, like "medieval itinerant students" or "solipsism," when on the other hand, if I went to buy something at the supermarket, words like sugar, flour or biscuit would leave me stumped. According to him, I couldn't claim to be able to speak German properly without first having familiarized myself with street slang like "garbage," "sulky," or "floozy." Even though M looked down on such things, I knew that what I needed was a course that would give me a thorough grounding in basic grammar. But when I brought this up with M she insisted that I also ought to master French through the same method she was advocating for German, and accused me of being crass, of acting like some Chinese exchange student who has to go back home if they fail the exam. But in the end, inevitably, M introduced me to an "artistic English and German teacher" whom she knew—Erich.

I could have gone to a private study school, which would have been cheaper, or even tried self-study; why didn't I? Instead, I followed M's recommendation and started meeting up with Erich twice a week. The lessons were really well put-together, and Erich's teaching method was genuinely effective, but I still wasn't easy to teach. I was only too aware of the kind of student I was—in all the years I'd spent at school, I'd never once given a lesson my full attention. Those sixteen years of formal education hadn't taught me a single thing. Thanks to my parents, I'd already mastered hangul and basic sums before I ever set foot in a classroom. Perhaps, like some kind of prodigy, I was already reading by myself at the age when most children are only stumbling through the alphabet. My parents took all this as a matter of course, and everything stemmed from there. Before long I was able to read books cover-to-cover, and ended up better acquainted with the pleasure of reading than that provided by school or friends. Once I started school I was forced to study the alphabet despite already knowing all the letters, which immediately put me off the lessons. In any case, these were little more than Spartan exercises in rote learning. I would sit there with my own book hidden inside the textbook, and after several years of this I'd lost all ability to even attempt to concentrate on what the teacher was saying. Even the most exciting topics fell on deaf ears. Meanwhile, the school curriculum progressed far beyond what little I'd picked up at home, moving on to topics which I hadn't a hope of understanding unless I paid attention in class, but by then the habit was too far ingrained, and I couldn't bring myself to concentrate even once the lessons stopped being mere repetitions of things I already knew. In less than two years I could only think of school as an endless progression of tedious, dragged-out hours, of feigned obedience and non-participation. The only way for me to get through each lesson was to read a book the whole time. Naturally, there was a limit to the number of books I could get my hands on, so it wasn't unusual for me to read the same book more than ten times. At first no one had any idea that I wasn't listening in class, because I always did the homework and my grades were generally above average. However, this was only possible because once I got home I would run through the things we'd been taught that day. This self-study became progressively less effective as the lessons increased in complexity. From a certain point onward the equations I was faced with remained completely impenetrable no matter how many times I went over them, and when the exam period came I had reams of notes to read, which, to make matters worse, were peppered with words that might as well have been written in a foreign language, and the free periods we were given at school simply weren't enough time for me to take in such an enormous amount of information. Instead of flowing on by, the everyday reality of school piled up on top of me, suffocating me under its oppressive weight. The lesson periods gradually became longer, and I spent those long hours battling anxiety and ennui as I sat there with my head bowed over the textbook, secretly engrossed in novels that I'd borrowed from the school library or saved up my pocket money to buy. After several rereads of the romance novels that all schoolgirls read at least once, like Louise Lynch, Jane Eyre, and the Anne of Green Gables series, I moved on to Dostoevsky and Tolstoy. These were followed by Thomas Mann and Heinrich Böll, Hemingway and Sartre, Kafka, Camus, but I can't really say that I genuinely *read* any of the books from that time; rather, they were simply something for my anxiety to worry away at. Besides, my reading list was determined by whichever old woodblock-printed editions I could get from the library. It made little difference to me whether I was poring over the minute type of Proust's *À la recherche*, some cheap romance novel, a graphic novel, *Judgment*, which had left me completely baffled, or *Lady Chatterley's Lover*. They were all just something to fill the time until the lesson was over. Because I couldn't concentrate on what was being said, because even the teacher's voice itself was nothing more than a string of meaningless sounds, I never understood a single thing, and eventually gave up all hope that I ever would. Before long, I was finding school almost impossible to bear. What had started out as a simple inability to concentrate during lessons gradually became more serious, and I was even making excuses to get out of physical education or art class, claiming that I wasn't feeling well or had forgotten to bring my materials. I opened my mouth as wide as everyone else during choir practice, but I was only miming. I never made a single friend, either, which could have injected at least a small amount of enjoyment into my experience of school. One day during class, the teacher came over and gave me two sharp raps on the shoulder with her pointer (my head was practically buried in my book), then pulled out the book I'd been concealing inside my textbook. She then announced my latest test scores in front of all the other students—the greatest punishment anyone could think of. She demanded to know why a student who had the temerity to do so poorly in a test, a test which, moreover, her own diligent teaching should have amply prepared that student for, had been reading a book instead of listening to the lesson. I don't remember the title now, but the book in question was some run-of-the-mill detective story. When I made no attempt at an answer, the teacher opened the book at random and started to read it out loud to the rest of the class; in the passage she read, the female proprietor of a dive bar was talking to the detective, in a suggestive, bantering way. If I remember correctly, their exchange had been fairly critical to the plot, containing a clue about how the investigation would turn out. It was the kind of thing that would satisfy an adolescent schoolgirl's keen sense of shame and morality. The other students all burst into laughter at the superficiality of the dialogue. Of course, the teacher laughed too. So this is the kind of thing you read! She curled her lip in contempt. And with your test scores never more than 70 at the very highest. Reading this nonsense, well, it's not appropriate, I'll have to confiscate it. You'd better watch yourself, now. Watch your attitude in my lessons. I'll make sure the other teachers know, too. That you were reading some trashy book during class, that is. We'll all have to make sure we keep a good eye on you. I'm no pushover! (This was one of her favorite threats, which she always delivered with a particular relish.) At the time, no one thought to ask me whether I wanted to keep on attending school—well, of course they didn't. The book was confiscated and I was made an example of, but I still carried on hiding my own books inside the textbooks, and I never did learn to listen in class, not even when I went to university. I couldn't listen, and so I couldn't understand. After graduation I never saw any of them again, my classmates. And there are things I can't grasp even now. Why do we have to go to school in order to learn things that we could learn just as well from reading books? The only thing school teaches us is how to submit to the will of the group, nothing more. Of course, unlike me, the majority of children don't yet know how to read when they start school. I've no idea how they manage to make it through school, keeping up the proper student lifestyle for all that time. In any case, there was no way I could learn German in anything resembling a school environment. Self-study would have been ideal, but given how very different German was from Korean I thought it might be a good idea to have a teacher, at least for the meantime. If school hadn't been such a nightmare for me I would have gone to a private academy, which felt less restrictive as it was up to you if and when you felt like dropping out.

Erich was a frequent player in my nightmare. He wears a long brown coat that comes all the way down to his ankles, reminding me of a kaftan, and a large hat that hides his face. He never used to dress so strangely when I knew him, but the mysterious logic of dreams means I instantly recognize him as Erich. He catches sight of me while reading the paper, then gets up and comes straight over to the table where I'm sitting. We're in some downtown café, packed with the weekend crowd, or else, perhaps, the smoking room in the national library.

"Long time no see. How've you been?" Always this same beginning. "I'm planning a birthday party next week; you'll come, won't you? You came last time, with M." He gets a ballpoint pen out of his pocket and writes the address on the memo pad the café provides for each table. And holds it out to me. Of course, this being a dream, I'm sitting there paralyzed, unable even to look away.

"How is M, anyway? I haven't seen her in ages. Are you two still together? Or don't you see her any more?"

And then, without even waiting for my answer, he whips around and disappears. And while all this is going on I just sit there staring at him, silent, transfixed. As if I'm chained to the seat. What agony it is. His pale, almost blond hair; his plain, conservative earring; his small, gray, inexpressive eyes; the lines around his serious-looking mouth; the skin of his face and neck, covered, if you look closely, with dense, fine, almost transparent hairs; even those guttural "r"s; in my dreams, I would encounter all these things quite distinctly. The dreams always unfolded in practically the same way. His clothing might be a little different, maybe instead of a hat he would be wearing big socks, or he might not use exactly the same words, but for the most part there would be no difference. He comes across me by chance, asks after M, disappears.

Erich was a great teacher. He was strict, always a positive quality for a teacher, but witty with it, and since he had experience with all kinds of students it never took him long to figure out how he should tailor his approach to each individual. He was also the only teacher whose first question was about what I actually wanted to get out of the lessons. When I told him I was hoping to be able to read, and eventually write, in German, he said "That might be impossible. But I guess we can try." This seemed neither unkind nor insulting, and in fact I considered it an uncommonly frank and intelligent response. Each week I would have one private lesson and one with two other students, both Chinese. I enjoyed these lessons, despite Erich's strictness, and even though there was a lot of homework it never felt like too much to cope with. Not getting on with your fellow students can be even worse than having an unsympathetic teacher, but the two Chinese students were even more of a pleasure to be around than Erich was. That was a happy time for me, which I suppose made me more inclined to be tolerant of others. I paid up-front for three months of lessons, and when we came to the third and final month Erich said "So, you told me you wanted to write in German; what shall we start with?"

I hesitated, suddenly aware that I would have to hand in anything I wrote to Erich. The mere prospect of another person reading through my error-strewn German was terrifying. But some things just need to be done, whether we like it or not.

"Well," I said, "I guess I just have to start writing. Simple as that. Right?"

So that's what I did, writing and submitting one German composition per week. Erich had the Chinese students translate Joyce's *The Dubliners* from English into German, one chunk at a time— their English was good, but they weren't interested in writing their own German compositions. Every time they made a fuss about it being too hard Erich reminded them that in Germany, this level of English text was used for high-school students. I chose to write about the zoo for my first piece, and took great pains over its structure and imagery. I called it "The Character Who Can Prove That They Are Going to the Zoo," and though I realized that such an unnaturally long title probably sounded a little odd, privately I flattered myself that it wasn't all that bad. But the moment Erich heard it he pulled a face and said that it didn't make sense, I'd have to edit it down. According to him those weren't the right words for the context, besides which the metaphor was clumsy. When he handed it back to me the whole thing was a mess of red ink, with only a bare handful of sentences having escaped unscathed. I can speak conspicuously (clearly). The hippopotamus is a woman who is unconnected to things (indifferent to things). It was dark (imprecise). I intend to strip off (free myself from) thoughts. I intend to sever from (break off with) you. Eventually you will become a post (part) of the scenery . . . Worst of all was the comment that Erich wrote in the margin: "content not clearly expressed." This was a terrible blow to my self-esteem, and after that I couldn't bring myself to show the piece to M. For my second piece, "Germans' Interior Decoration," I made an effort to keep my sentences relatively short and not use any expression that I didn't fully understand. The piece that resulted was so unbearably banal it could well have been written by a child at kindergarten, yet, and despite the many errors it still contained, Erich showered it with praise. But it was shame, not pride, that I felt. The piece was nothing but a collection of incomparably commonplace, meaningless statements, exactly the kind of writing I hated—really, truly, hated. Normally I couldn't stand anything that "read easily," and I'd only written it like that in order to avoid making too many errors and confusing the reader. The very act of writing it felt like I'd physically injured myself. And yet, with all that said, I'd gone ahead and written it all the same. It was only ever intended for me to practice forming simple sentences, not stun anyone with its literary perfection; it had about as much of the latter as did the mangled ad phrases at a Chinese takeaway. The worst thing was that Erich had introduced me to the Chinese students as "a writer in her home country." Naturally, this was of no great concern to them, but it made me even more acutely aware of the wretchedness of what I'd written. It was even more embarrassing than the first, error-strewn piece, which Erich had criticized for its "absolutely incomprehensible" German. After these initial knocks to my self-esteem, I began to write about M.

I'm not sure what prompted the decision to write about M. Our relationship was hardly a suitable theme for German-language homework, though of course, I told myself, I needn't necessarily put down every reckless thought and unbridled emotion that sprang into my mind. But the desire to write, the blazing desire to set down sentences that were true, sincere, and not the stuff of children, eventually won out over circumspection. Perhaps I just wanted to show Erich that I could write something other than clumsy descriptive pieces larded with senseless, immature words, something that could never be accused of having anything one could label "content." However it was, an uncontrollable flood of strength carried me straight from the first sentence to the last. I remember the evening I wrote it. M was in the bedroom and I was writing in her living room. For dinner we had instant pasta with mozzarella and basil, the kind that you can just pour water in and boil. If you like, you can add a lump of butter to the water as it boils, and mix some powdered tomato sauce in with the pasta. Neither M nor I were fond of cooking. M's aversion was a little more serious than mine, so that even having to add a few vegetables, like boiled potatoes, chiles, or cabbage, seemed like too much fuss over nothing. On top of that she spent quite a while as a strict vegetarian, and wouldn't even allow herself shrimp or smoked salmon with the pasta. M was terribly emaciated. Rather than being naturally small-boned, it was just that there wasn't an ounce of excess fat on her, no unnecessary softness rounding out her body. That body began at her cheekbones, their flat planes strikingly exotic, almost like those of a Finn, and at her pale, wide forehead. M was tall, with a fairly broad chest; her pelvis was narrow, and her legs were long and slender. Her skin was a pale, matte white. There was nothing sensuous or voluptuous about her body, partly because it didn't serve for such things, but mainly because she was just so thin. M herself would never acknowledge this, though, and whenever she gained any weight would immediately claim that she needed to lose at least five kilos. I, on the other hand, had a much more healthy appetite, and could never get rid of the habit of adding plenty of butter when I made pasta. I left the lid off while I boiled the pasta, so the kitchen floor and the cupboard handles became slippery with grease, and the smell of buttery tomato sauce spread through the whole house. The only way to get rid of it was to open the window in the living room, where we ate. That evening the weather was bitterly cold, so M, who risked suffering a potentially fatal asthma attack if she caught a cold, took *The Complete Correspondence of Clara and Robert Schumann* to read in the bedroom. The first time we met we shook hands, and I'd been struck by how long and inflexible M's hand was, almost like a fish, while the skin of her palm had seemed unusually rough and dry. Later she told me that as a teenager, almost every year in early summer her palms would crack, fissuring into excruciating wounds that became inflamed, then covered over with proud flesh. And then there are M's blue-gray eyes. Those eyes each like a winter lake with an iceberg at its heart, its perfect stillness undisturbed by waterfowl, fish, or even a single wavering blade of grass, eyes that crystallized in a single gaze the most sublime perfection of silence. In an orchestra, M said, I am the piano, and you are the contrabass. I couldn't not write about M.

Erich praised the piece about M too, but in a fairly perfunctory way, so I assumed he was simply being polite. The meticulous red-inked corrections were still there, though there were far fewer errors overall than for any of the previous pieces, and none of them were really that significant. And that was the sum total of the feedback I received. I always looked forward to Erich's comments, particularly when he set the grammatical issues aside and gave me his own personal response to the piece, or asked about possible subjects for future compositions. But when it came to the final piece, the one about M, there was none of that; instead, Erich invited M and I to his birthday party the following week. The other guests were all current or former students of his, their friends, plus his own friends and colleagues. All the students at the party insisted on talking to him in English rather than German, including the two Chinese students I shared my classes with. Two tables had been set out in the kitchen, one for vegetarians and the other for those who ate meat. The food was all delicious, the company uniformly friendly and intelligent. Up until then I'd only ever seen Erich in the guise of a no-nonsense teacher, one whose strict discipline even tended to make his students nervous, but at the party I was shocked to find him playing the jester—he was even wearing a red Pierrot mask! To me this was all extremely incongruous, but according to M he'd always had a playful side, you just had to catch him in the right mood. M and I stood by the vegetarian table eating ice cream, arm in arm under the faint glow of the kitchen lights. It would have been rude to try and cut into other people's conversations, so I preferred to just hover on the edges, trying to make my presence seem as natural as possible. M had promised not to leave me alone if she could help it. Just then, the sheer joy of having met M, how utterly unique she was, and the fact that she felt the same about me, thrilled through me in such a powerful, unprecedented rush that I impulsively pressed my lips to the back of M's hand. M reached over with her other hand and grasped mine. I felt my cheeks flush hot, and thoughts of the future flashed through my mind. Who could tell what might happen? Then Erich waved both arms at me from the other side of the corridor where he was surrounded by a gaggle of students, calling out "Hey, the guys are *here*! All the men worth putting out for"—this was a fairly crude expression which I only knew thanks to Joachim, and I remember being shocked to hear Erich use it—"are over here, so what are you doing over there? Come and mingle!"

7) Love is easily negated, and always imprisoned in a haze of obscurity; it can be shallow, wounding, irresponsible and shameless, constantly making excuses for itself. Long after having dwindled to nothingness it can still be found waiting in the wings, grimly intent on any opportunity to speak itself back into existence—even more self-obsessed than some simpering woman giggling about how she's ruined her figure by getting herself knocked up—and worst of all is the way it drones on, oblivious to the existence of anything outside itself, that tedious voice that gets forgotten so quickly it's almost embarrassing, its memory fading swifter than the beauty of roses in full bloom. It's nothing, it was nothing from the first, and later on it was even more nothing. I'm resting my head on M's chest, listening to the footsteps of the cold, cold rain as it falls on the empty fields, the fields that we drove through to get here. The rustle of dry grass, a wood's purple shadow streaked across the horizon, the tracks of wild animals, the exposed flesh of a tree where a branch has been cut off, bare feet

shocked blue with cold, the seemingly indecipherable slant of M's damp eyebrows, the rose that grew in M's aunt's garden, the two small graves, the garden pond, the stubby apple trees.

M pointed out her favorite plates, which dated from well before the war. When she stayed here as a child, she said, they'd always been reserved for her especial use. A bookcase filled a whole wall in the living room, but it was almost bare; her uncles must have thrown out all the books and records that M remembered so fondly. All that remained was an encyclopedia so old it was only of use as a museum piece, a box full of typed manuscripts, theater scripts written in an old-fashioned hand, an illustrated *Gone with the Wind*, a bundle of old magazines with curling, yellowed pages, books by writers now dead and almost completely unknown, a thirty-year-old volume on the theory of stage directing, and a rather shabby-looking collection of Buchner's plays. These were the unclaimed relics. M's aunt had been a playwright—apparently, she'd been quite well-known at one time. The last time the two of them had seen each other was when M was six, and her parents had left her here while they went traveling to East Asia. It wasn't the first time she'd been left with her aunt like that, but M's parents got divorced shortly after that particular trip and never went traveling again, not even by themselves, so M never saw her aunt again. With being so young at the time, M's only memory of her aunt was of an old woman who'd really hated it if M didn't eat her soup in absolute silence, scolding her into frightened obedience. The window in the study looked out over the garden, with its two small graves and its apple trees. The graves were dogs' graves. M wanted us to take a stroll around the garden, barefoot. The rain was coming down continuously, and the ground was hard and cold. The distant woods, the horizon knuckled by low hills, the signpost informing us of the name of the street and the location of the post office, and the gently sloping road—this was all that was visible to the eye. We were barely a few dozen kilometers from the city but the houses were almost all single-story, the tallest things around being a handful of huge barns. But in their yards there was no sign of anything living, and even the road had nowhere to go except over the hills and into the sky; in fact the sky was almost all there was, the sky and the falling rain. The only other moving thing was a yellow postal van. I watched as the van receded into the distance, moving away up the road's gentle slope until it disappeared altogether, and the vibrating waves of silence seemed to have absorbed the last audible traces of its existence. M was lying down on the chaise longue, eyes closed, both hands on her chest. Her breathing had a ragged edge to it. I got a dry towel from the bathroom cupboard and rubbed her bare feet.

That was a happy time for me. That whole period of my life seems to have passed by in a flash, but if asked whether my happiness was purely the result of being with M, I would have to say yes, it was. I spent a long time trying to deny that fact, but without success. Now, though, the only place where that happiness still remains is in fossilized memories. Memories of M, of course, but the M that exists within them is not the real M. As time passes, the gap between the two grows ever wider. The former lacks physical form, doesn't interact with me, isn't even aware of me, and though its outer appearance resembles M's, even down to the clothes it wears and the way it shapes a gesture, this is only superficial, utterly meaningless. That thing is not M. In time, those memories hardened in such a way that the M who lived within them ended up as a composite of all characteristics most unlike those of the M who really exists. That's just the way it turned out. And now I can't even claim to know her any more. Absolutely not, not by any means.

We were both equally unaware of our respective pasts, and gave no real thought to the future. Past and future; their very existence is tinged with sadness, revealing, as they do, both irrevocable mistakes and unavoidable oblivion. M would frequently work herself up into a passion, knowing that when next spring came I would no longer be eligible to stay in the country, and would have to go back home. It was difficult for M to just quietly acquiesce to this, a phenomenon that she saw as highly irrational. Perhaps the difficulty was partly due to her lack of experience with this type of situation. Not all of us live like nomads, after all. Her fragile health meant she'd never strayed very far from the city where she'd been born and raised. I wasn't actually all that different—I, too, had never formed such an intimate relationship with someone living in a distant country, and the thought of us ending up thousands of kilometers apart left me equally at a loss. It was a difficult situation all around, especially given M's emotional response whenever I tried to broach the topic of my departure. Yes, I would have to leave, but I tried to assure her that soon afterward, at the earliest opportunity, in fact, I would come back. The only problem was that there was no way of knowing when that earliest opportunity might be. There would be all sorts of things that needed sorting out when I got back to Korea, things that might well keep me tied up there for some time, so that I couldn't say with any certainty when I would be coming back. I could understand M's frustration, her anger. It was impossible for M to go to Korea, where it might be difficult to obtain the medicine she needed, much less find a GP specializing in her allergies. Not to mention the various endemic diseases that were no doubt particular to the country. But none of this altered the fact that I had to go, and my firmness—some might call it cruelty—in explaining this to M had hurt her deeply. The way I saw it, there was simply no other option. M insisted I could work around the entry visa by leaving Germany only briefly—I could stay with her stepsister in Paris—but while this would take care of the most obvious and immediate issue, the more fundamental ones would still be left unsolved. If I wanted to stay in Germany long-term, things had now reached the point where I really needed to start tying up the various loose ends I'd left behind me in Korea. Some of these were financial, and could only be dealt with in person at the bank; then, if I wanted to permanently relocate from Korea to Germany, I'd first need to go and reclaim all the belongings I'd put in storage. Three or four months, at the most, would probably be sufficient. But potential problems mounted up, one following the other: the bank might not loan me all the money I needed, I might not be able to find somewhere suitable to move into, or a new place to store all my things; the process of finding a flat and moving might take longer than I anticipated, or end up costing far more than I'd initially factored in, so really, how could I be expected to make even a rough estimate of how much time I was going to need? It was less the number of different things that needed sorting out, and more that what did need doing had been left completely up in the air. I could have gone ahead and told M "three or four months at the most," but it wasn't a promise I could be sure of keeping. I never discussed this with M in any real detail. They were my problems, for one, and it was really money that lay at the root of them. Besides, if I tried to go into detail then my sentences would end up getting longer and longer, with even the slightest grammatical error opening the door for uncertainty or misunderstanding to creep in, and I'd have to keep qualifying myself, explaining my explanation, the shabby rags of my words piling up in a dizzying accumulation, guilt and shame rising up in me even as I tried to explain this guilt away. In the face of all this, M would eventually be forced to accept that I had to go, that

I had to go without setting a precise date for my return, and that there was nothing she could do to stop me. But though I would have succeeded in forcing her acceptance, it would be at the cost of giving her the impression that I was doing all this deliberately, that my decision to leave was the result of a conscious choice rather than necessity forcing my hand, and that all my talk was just one excuse after another, a litany of self-justification; the thing is, what I'm trying to say, which added no new information and would only serve to make her think that I was one of those puffed-up, permanently unsatisfied egoists who swell the ranks of the lower-middle class. I didn't want that. There was nothing M could gain from such a spiel, no response it could elicit aside from simple acquiescence. I would miss her, oh, as soon as I stepped onto the plane, and was merely thinking of all the preparations I'd need to make in order to come back to her, and, if possible, to stay for slightly longer next time. I told M all this; she couldn't help but interpret it as nothing more than that polite farewell dictated by convention, a mere kindness on the part of the one who is leaving toward the one being left behind. But wasn't there perhaps another reason for my wanting to go back to Korea? Wasn't I also worried about my relationship with M, a relationship, after all, which had come about so quickly I'd almost been taken by surprise? Did the prospect of long-term love not perhaps fill me with unease, and wasn't I hoping to put some distance between myself and this love, just for a little while? Just as M feared being left alone in Berlin, wasn't I worried about being left alone in love? These doubts roiled inside me, but I never let so much as a hint at them pass my lips. If M announced one day that she was going to pack her bags and leave for some distant country, abandoning me here in Berlin, saying I will always love you, but, and I honestly want to come back as soon as possible, but, the thing is, you see, I just can't make any definite promises; if our roles were reversed, how could I even express the agony I know I'd feel? The transfixing pain of a shaft of ice cast by a frozen autumn day, the internal conflict between doubting love and simultaneously craving it, desperately seeking constant assurances, fear of being abandoned, envy toward the one who is free to leave, the suffocating premonition that the moment will come when our love will be lost, when we become strangers to each other, knowing, at the end of our love, no more of each other than we had done before its first stirrings, and worst of all is that none of this will have the power to move me any more, to produce even the faintest pang of regret. Eventually, there was one argument when instead of responding to the point I'd raised, M simply turned to gaze out of the window. After that, she never raised the subject again. She didn't get angry, didn't swear, stopped trying to calculate the earliest possible date of my return, stopped sighing out loud and pestering me with questions. All she said, quite quietly, was that she understood my situation and accepted that I had to leave. Nothing else had changed. I know now how deeply hurt she must have been.

Contrary to Joachim's insistence, M wasn't rich. To Joachim, born into a working-class family, someone like M who managed to get by without full-time employment must surely have some vast source of private wealth. This assumption was cemented by the fact that M frequently attended pricey music recitals and didn't begrudge spending money on books or records, but all the same it wasn't correct. The house she lived in was owned by her mother, so she only had to pay a nominal amount of rent, and while it was true that she wasn't employed full-time she worked in the research room at the language institute three days a week, and occasionally, under a pen name, had essays on twentieth-century music published in magazines. M had something of an inferiority complex when it came to those who did manual labor. Whenever she experienced financial difficulties, such as during university when her application for a government grant was rejected because of her parents' assets, M envied those around her who could self-fund by taking on some kind of physical work. To me, M's lifestyle actually seemed very frugal, given that she didn't go out unless she had to and never spent money on makeup or jewelry. Rather than a conscious effort to economize, M's attitude toward spending money seemed more like the result of long habit. In fact, considering she relied on my tuition fees—hardly substantial—to cover her living costs, there was really no reason for Joachim to think of her as rich. Just because someone says they would happily spend ten day's income, no, more than that even, to hear the Budapest Strings Chamber Orchestra perform Bartók's string quartets, that doesn't necessarily make them "rich." You can't simply assume that attend-

ing a visiting professor's lectures on linguistics, during which the blackboard gets covered with a prosodic structure chain every bit as incomprehensible as ancient Egyptian hieroglyphs, an incomprehensibility further compounded by the said professor's relentless chatter, is an extravagant pleasure, the preserve of those social classes for whom money is no object, especially when the person involved has entirely relinquished hotel stays, a car, and expensive clothes, or else was already entirely indifferent to such things. I wandered here and there through the halls of memory, searching for proof that M was neither rich nor a member of the leisure classes. What I really wanted was to bring M into stark relief as a discrete, specific entity, to establish our innocence; I couldn't bring myself to acknowledge that our relationship was purely the product of chance, of one human being's indiscriminate—or worse: prejudiced—use of their free will. I didn't matter what Joachim thought. M wasn't rich—she couldn't be. In rummaging through old memories, I was trying to rid myself of the suspicion that M had only deigned to notice me because she was rich and unconstrained, the holder of a linguistics degree, easily taken up by whatever was novel, a voracious reader and culture obsessive who'd become unconsciously influenced by Asian mysticism, which had led her to adopt an air of tranquility, stripping her words and gestures of all superfluity, and maintaining a fairly limited social circle, and because of all this taken together was after a partner whose intellectual soil would provide her with continuous stimulation. Joachim could load a single sentence with all of these implications.

"I mean, rich people like M are naturally after a certain type, and you just happened to be it, that's all."

Plagued with doubts, love slowly lost its vitality, became an enfeebled shadow of its former self. Fear of opening my mouth, fear of certain questions being asked, fear of suspicions becoming reality, fear of revealing too much of myself without this being reciprocated. And so yes, there was a time, only a brief period, when I'd wanted to take a good, objective look at the two of us, something that would only be possible if we took a break from our relationship. After I'd finished rubbing M's feet dry, I sat on the floor, leaned my head against her chest and listened to the beating of her heart. My hair was damp with rain; M held me tightly to her. How long did we remain like this, was it a huge stretch of time or no more than an instant, were we inside that time or watching it sweep past us; held by each other's gaze, had the "memory us" managed to resist this passage of time, the headaches and slight fevers that mark the coming of old age, the slow yet inexorable weathering of our once-distinct outlines, or had we grown further apart, a slow descent into lethargy, watching each other from opposite sides of a window, our fists thudding dull against the glass? My fingers glided over M's breasts, those ribs whose stubborn elegance called to mind that of a stag, her smooth, feverish stomach and goose-pimpled arms. Tender, tender M. It seems I will endure and you cannot, until, finally, those positions are reversed.

Erich came over, slung an arm around each of our shoulders, and studied our faces in turn. His lip twitched, almost a sneer, but perhaps just a spasm. He seemed about to say something, though I had no idea what. He'd been drinking, that much was certain, but you couldn't really say he was drunk. He wasn't the kind of person who would drink to excess. There'd clearly been something he wanted to say when he came over, but now he'd changed his mind, making do with a nod to M and the announcement that my last homework piece had been "really great."

"Oh, really? What was it about?" M asked.

"Oh, just, internal feelings . . . something about poetry . . . and music, you know. I thought I knew you from somewhere; d'you mean we've never met? If she keeps at it, there's no reason she couldn't get something published here, just like Yoko Tawada. No? But then," he turned to me, "I'm not sure why Yoko Tawada feels she has to write in German, so I don't really understand about you, either."

M placed her hand lightly on Erich's arm and spoke to him as if to a child.

"Language, Erich, that is not mere art, but mind, is far more universal than you think. It transcends racial differences, even those between individuals—" But Erich seemed to think M was joking.

"Even if I accepted your idealism, it still doesn't explain what this 'wandering in search of a universal mind' is all for. Is it really just something you've plucked out of Schubert's songs?"

No matter what view you hold regarding his sexual inclinations, August von Platen left behind some truly passionate, sorrowful poetry. At the close of his poem "From Tristan and Isolde" he writes:

> What he desired never came to pass
> And the hours, spinning out the thread of life,
> Are only murderers, set to kill him:
> What he longs for, he will never obtain,
> What he desired never came to pass.

Schubert set two volumes of von Platen's poems to music; from those two, he clearly thought Platen's poetry very well suited to the theme of winter. In fact, these songs seem to preempt "Winter Journey." One of them is called "You Do Not Love Me." It begins like this:

> My heart is torn to pieces, you do not love me!

Those who accord biography a privileged position in interpreting a writer's work might give the following reading: the poet had a lover, the darling of his heart whom none could ever replace, but this love was unrequited, and so the poet, having been forced to tear himself away from his personal Narcissus, and feeling as though his heart was truly being torn apart, is singing of his grief and loneliness. Certain people would even insist that in the final stanza—"Wherefore do the narcissus flowers bloom? You do not love me!"—the narcissus, being the flower which most reveals the sublime beauty of young masculinity, symbolizes the gender of the poet's lover.

Later on, at a private recital hosted by a passionate Schubert fan, I had the opportunity to hear that song sung exactly as it should be. The Belgian singer stood by a chair, made sure she had the right note with the aid of the piano, then produced a deep, low-pitched tone as the very first syllable of the song. My heart, at first those were the only words I heard. When she articulated the phrase, her hands, which she'd been holding near her waist, moved upward as if pulled by the rising pitch of her voice; this happened repeatedly throughout the performance. I was sitting very near to the singer, so was able to catch all the subtle modulations of her voice. And Erich had begun in exactly the same way, my heart. He must have been remembering the Schubert song that I'd used in my composition.

"My heart, my heart is torn to pieces, you do not love me. You said to me, you do not love me. Although I beg, implore, entreat your love, you do not love me . . ."

Erich stopped there, leaving me with the odd sense of having been insulted, a feeling which chilled me to the core. I couldn't say for sure whether that had been Erich's intention, but that was certainly how it felt. But why? Because he'd been drinking? Because, given I knew full well his opinion of her, his mention of Yoko Tawada as another Asian writer who chose to write in German couldn't help but come across as barbed? He'd cited her example a couple times in class, while discussing an article called "Escaping Asians" with the Chinese students. His opinion was actually quite neutral, and mildly expressed, but it was still clear that he didn't think highly of her writing. "So I don't really understand about you, either," he'd said. Was that mockery? Did I feel insulted because he'd read aloud, quite calmly and in front of M, the Schubert song I'd used? Erich had always thought of me as weak. He'd never said it in so many words, but his attitude allowed me to make an educated guess. The universality of interior language was a matter of perfect indifference to him. I was a student learning a language, and given the inferior mental world that is all such a thing, "a student learning a language," is able to spread open and present to the world, I was weak. In the Schubert song Erich saw an analogy to my relationship with M. But that wasn't what had made me feel insulted. He was entitled to his conjectures, it wasn't rude, and he hadn't insulted me by conceiving of it. I'd written the piece, he'd corrected it, and there was nothing I could do about it. Erich was a passionate, indefatigable teacher of English and German, and of all the teachers I'd known he was both the strictest and the most effective. That was just the way he was.

In the tram on the way home M asked if I was angry at Erich. No, I said, I wasn't. Yes, he'd slighted my composition, but I myself knew there was nothing wrong with it, and I had no desire to keep on criticizing him. M seemed to hesitate for a moment, then said that though Erich could come across as extremely cold, he'd always known how to deal with students fairly and objectively, so I shouldn't judge him too severely. She was clearly trying to defend him, but also, perhaps unconsciously, herself. We both turned to look out of the window for a while. M had pulled her scarf all the way up to her mouth, to protect her from the intense cold of the unheated tram. So when she finally added that, purely out of basic physical curiosity, an act which held absolutely no significance whatsoever, she had slept with Erich, her words were so muffled I could barely make them out.

After the recital was over, the Schubert devotee addressed the gathering.

"It's a well-known fact that Franz Schubert lived a short and unhappy life, even in comparison with the lives of other artists. He remained obscure and impoverished all his life, and the worst thing of all was that he was short and fat. If you look at the portraits we have of him, rather than simply admitting that he was not a handsome man, one could even go so far as to say that he looks somehow ponderous; ludicrous, almost. His fingers, we are told, were 'short and thick,' quite unbefitting a pianist; he'd always been severely shortsighted, and he became even more unattractive with age, developing the bloated physique of a gourmand. It goes without saying that he had absolutely no luck with women. We even have it on record that he was admitted to the hospital with venereal disease. The song 'Winter Journey' was dismissed even when it was first given a name, but Schubert himself maintained that he loved this work more than any other, and that one day the critics would come around to his point of view. He'd always been accustomed to being slighted, and he never did succeed in securing a patron, though perhaps he didn't want to, perhaps the kind of life where one's only legacy is some shabby old clothes and a quilt was the only life that was really right for him. He was an inveterate reader and a sensitive, repressed romanticist. All that comes across in the records is a short, fat, shy myopic, a penniless youth who, when pierced through by the passion of music, didn't know how to express it and trembled like someone trying and failing to suppress laughter, someone whose weak eyesight meant he was constantly flinching. But, as Hölderlin said, we are nothing ourselves, that which we pursue is our all, and Schubert's music, some of which we have just heard, was his all, just as it is for myself and all who love it; a pleasure that speaks with the whole soul, both Genesis and Revelations, the beginning and end of this world."

The Schubert devotee continued with her address. Eight years ago after discovering Schubert's music, this thing she loved above all else, it was as though the scales had finally fallen from her eyes, the previously baffling vagaries of the heart resolved into a sublime symphony, and Nijinsky in his costume of yellow silk became the stars, frozen in the heavens above time's vista, and when she first encountered that starlight shining in the sky, she drifted away along with the light, into the fine-grained matter of the distant universe, where nobody would ever find her.

8) There was still a bit of time left before I had to leave the country, but I decided to break it off with M there and then. While she was at the university doing some research I packed all my things into two bags, and whatever wouldn't fit I threw into the trash. It would be a lie if I said that I hadn't been frightened at the prospect of returning to Korea alone. But I had no choice. In no sense am I proud of how I behaved back then: I hesitated, vacillated, decided to cut myself a bit of slack, tried to predict other people's actions, weighed up the pros and cons of every decision. When I first arrived in Germany I'd taken out a one-year rental contract for a room in a shared house; the place had been gathering dust since I'd moved in with M, but at least it meant I had somewhere of my own to go back to. The next day I decided to go straight to the airport and reserve a seat on a flight to Korea. It felt as though I'd gone full circle, returning to the same situation I'd been in when I first arrived in Germany. I didn't know M, in fact I'd never even met her. I found myself truly sickened by this city, these streets, by every aspect of the outside world, which seemed to be constantly importuning me, and once back home I planned to pick up the thread of my old life, a life spent reading and listening to music.

As time passed, I became seized with doubt. What could have made me freeze like that? Lying in the bed beside M, I listened to the night spreading itself around us, feeling like the end of something. I waited until M was sleeping, but couldn't fall asleep myself. There were no questions I could ask, and besides, I didn't even want to listen to whatever she might have to say. So I began to interrogate myself instead. What was this desire for possession that had taken hold of me? Where had it come from, and could I really carry on being burdened by its oppressive weight? Beauty, delicacy, concern and generosity, peaceful seclusion, reading, music, and writing . . . and the union of two souls, found after so long; was it right to have betrayed and destroyed all those things in the work of an instant? Why do humans have this desire for possession, and why do we grow savage when we cannot satisfy it? The strains of a single melody, slowly and agonizingly teased from among a thousand other sounds only for its sublime order to be destroyed by a moment's anger, tearing it down and trampling it underfoot

96 so that it can never be made whole again, calling down clichéd curses on itself and displaying its ugliness to the world as it rends its flesh like a crazed chicken, how can we simply remain indifferent to all this? Why can we do nothing about it? Where does the desire for possession come from? Why does it spit at and ridicule all the ethical questions proposed in the course of long reflection, a journey undertaken within our innermost selves? If it can't be controlled, then what is there that's left for us to do; no, given that it can't be controlled, what else of value can human beings ever hope to achieve? M had managed to come out of the whole thing unscathed—this thing which she claimed had meant nothing, the product of nothing more than a basic and purely physical curiosity—she was still as beautiful as ever, but the same couldn't be said for me. M might have been deaf to the sound of her world collapsing, but not me. Had she been trying to get revenge? Perhaps, so that our positions might be reversed and she would no longer be

the one left behind, she'd decided to be the one to make the break.
A further torrent of questions poured forth. If M's soul was with
me then why did Erich need to be a problem, if mere flesh, limited
and inconsistent, really did amount to nothing, then why did I
have to suffer on account of their one-night stand, why couldn't
I break free of this permanently unsatisfied desire for possession,
when I was only too aware of how utterly base it was? I couldn't
come up with a single word of consolation or justification for
myself. When its corollary is a hunger to monopolize M's gestures,
her shadow, her voice, love soon becomes a hell. This is how M
made me suffer. M, M would eventually discover this.

But perhaps my problem wasn't solely the desire for possession.
I couldn't forgive myself for having been so rash, couldn't believe
I'd been foolish enough to show the composition to anyone else, let
alone Erich. With hindsight, my sense of shame was overwhelm-
ing, and perhaps this shame was the real reason that I couldn't bring
myself to forgive M. She too had played a part in Erich's mockery,
albeit unintentionally. I saw them from within my shame, saw her
mouth hanging open as she laughed at the stream of filthy words
issuing from his. I saw M mince up to Erich, swaying her hips
like a streetwalker, and perch on his knee to read my composition,
assuming an obscene position with the easy air of long familiarity.
I read all this in M's sleeping face, in the even cadences of her
breathing, and all that I'd once found there, universal grammar
and the language of barbarians, all that beautiful, sublime meaning which had been transmuted into sentences and songs, thus to
find its way to me, had disappeared without the slightest flicker of
protest. After that, all that was left behind was a shriveled, barren
face, the face of a stranger. My shame made me blanch and shiver
in the darkness. I was still breathing, but in every other sense I
was no different from a corpse. I was buried, my heart was buried

deep underground. But that sense of shame was still as strong as ever. Surely it was this that was causing me such anguish, my own painful awareness of this feeling within myself. In other words, that keen sense of shame was exacerbated by my continually dwelling on it, my belief that it was inevitable. That swamp of shame eventually subsumed me, rendered me null and meaningless, so all that existed was shame reflected between two mirrors, the infinite repetition of that image. My own actions were the root cause of this shame, having directly prompted the event that was causing me such agony; naturally, this made me feel ashamed, painfully aware of my own shamefulness, still more ashamed by my inability to conceal this feeling, the shame itself strangely less unbearable than the fact of my feeling ashamed, and eventually, within all that senselessness, I discovered that I'm the kind of person who is ashamed of shame itself. Taking it one step further, the other thing I found out was that of the three of us, the truly sickening, unforgivable and incomparably superficial one was neither M nor Erich, but me. I lay awake the whole night, trembling with the burden of this knowledge. At one point it occurred to me that perhaps it was all a lie, that M had lied about sleeping with Erich because she was angry at my determination to return to Korea. But then I realized that no, this idea of mine was the only lie, something I'd dreamt up in an attempt to preserve my self-respect. The look in M's eyes when she'd said those words—purely out of basic physical curiosity, she'd said, and her eyes had confirmed the truth of this. Purely out of basic physical curiosity. This phrase clearly hadn't just popped out on the spur of the moment; rather, it must have been planned in advance, the wording carefully calculated to inflict the deepest wound. "Basic physical curiosity" served to emphasize Erich's masculinity, the fact that he, or more specifically his penis, could provide the regular pleasures sought by regular women.

But I knew M too well for those words to succeed in making me envy Erich. She never had, and she never would. Penetrative sex with a man was not where M's inclinations lay, and she couldn't trick me into thinking otherwise. M was far too independent, far too asexual, far too strong, far too defiant, to get much from the simple pleasures of male-female sex. Even now, when I've already forgotten so much, I can at least remember that about her. In the bedroom, Erich would have been nothing more than a vibrator for M, whatever words he might have whispered having no more import than the machine's quiet hum. Of that much I was certain. At least, that was what I claimed to believe, what I desperately tried to convince myself of. And still I slipped back into despair, and started confronting M over her moral stance. But when you slept together, purely out of this basic physical curiosity, didn't you feel a sense of shame? Some kind of moral aversion? Did you consider, at all, the estrangement of mind from flesh? It wasn't like that. It wasn't like that at all. I see no reason for physical relations to be held sacred, especially when pleasure is their sole purpose. This was a long-held belief of mine, dating from my teenage years. I've never been able to understand relationships where the couple's intimacy depends on the merely physical. With all that in mind, why did I feel unable to go on living with M?

M looked to be sound asleep that night, but perhaps she was only pretending.

9) I refused to open the door even after M had rung the bell several times and begged me to let her in. M spent the whole night huddled on the doorstep of the house I'd moved back into, and the next morning an ambulance had to come and pick her up. By the time she arrived at the hospital, one of her knees had

apparently swollen to almost double its usual size. I'd stayed inside the house the whole time, listening as she hung on the bell and pounded on the door. At first I thought that this was the perfect way to part from her, but at the same time I wanted to stay with her forever, just like this, as was only possible like this. If I opened the door and let her in that would already be to admit defeat, and once I allowed her to engage me in conversation there would be no going back. It would all end in disaster, as much of a mistake as the one I'd made in submitting that composition to Erich. In your haste, in your certainty, you'll often find yourself betrayed by the most extraneous, superficial facts. Besides, I was angry with her. More than anything else, though, I simply couldn't forgive myself, any more than I could forgive M. At the time, it seemed like the suffering I'd brought down on M had been turned around and was punishing me, too. But after that long night was over, the world was restored to its previous form. I made the conscious decision to stop obsessing over happiness, satisfaction, passion, my ego. Clinging to unanswerable questions, getting lost in endless chains of logic, wasn't the way to end this suffering. Instead, I gave myself over completely to the circumstances in which I found myself. I was standing in the middle of a sea of dark red soil. The soaring pillars which lined both sides of the road were inscribed with records of some ancient victory, part of a triumphal highway now lying forgotten somewhere deep in the desert. But the deadly sandstorms, the wars of past millennia left me unmoved. It was neither hope nor despair that impelled me along the road, but the simple desire to leave that place. Nowhere was there even the slightest trace of human life. I walked between those dreary, crumbling pillars, each bolstered by an equally dreary temple, past Palmyra's Roman theater, its marble-clad splendor long forgotten, replaced by a scene of decayed grandeur currently being scoured by a great dust storm whose fine-grained winds were torched red by the last faint rays of the setting sun. I walked on all the way to the valley of the tombs, when suddenly, so suddenly that I was shaken out of my composure, the road vanished from underneath my feet. After breaking up with M I'd somehow been transported, finding myself in the middle of that incomparable desert vista, then shortly afterward I'd turned a corner that didn't exist, stepping out of the ruins of ancient Palmyra straight into a bustling shopping center at Christmastime. The temptation to start plaguing myself with questions was there, but I resisted.

M's knee was still full of pus at our final meeting, making her walk with a limp. Her voice was calm, but the deep shadows below her eyes told of sleepless nights. All those long hours she'd spent huddled outside my door. A sub-zero night, and with despair pushing her to the brink of exhaustion, yet somehow she got away with nothing more serious than a swollen knee. They told her she'd have to use a wheelchair for a while, and rest up until she recovered her strength. She was in the hospital for a month, and as soon as she was discharged she came to see me, hobbling on her crutches. We drank tea together. According to the lunar calendar we were already in spring, but the days were still cold. I opened a window to let the air circulate, hung my laundry up to dry in the bathroom, and the whole house seemed instantly refreshed. We spoke about music, our comments brief and desultory. A beautiful, light Mendelssohn piece came on the radio, and afterward I put on Bach's "canon" suites, a recent purchase. The suites were based on a single musical theme given to Bach by King Frederick as a challenge for improvisation, when he'd visited the king at Potsdam in 1747. This "Musical Offering," made up of canons, fugues, and a trio of sonatas, was the first of Bach's many compositions that really appealed to me. Later on, though, I was incredibly disappointed to learn that it was an "offering" in the religious sense of "sacrifice"—this, apparently, was where the word derived from—with the king as its recipient. Bach died in 1750. He composed this "Musical Offering" in his final year. The records say that he knew his death was approaching so decided to put the finishing touches to his life as a musician by revising his works for publication. I wrote a short essay about Bach and the "Musical Offering." I'd always longed to write something about music, if the opportunity ever arose. When I discussed it with M, she suggested that I could look at some of her own articles on Bach's final works, and even offered to bring me the relevant magazines, but I told her firmly that there was no need. I explained that I wasn't intending to write a specialist article about music, like hers. I began the piece with a general-interest discussion of Wittgenstein—a great fan of Bach's—and planned to finish it with the visit to King Frederick's Sanssouci Palace. Still in its incomplete

form, I made a rough translation into German and read this out to M. The translation was clumsy beyond belief, but still M gave it her full attention, listening patiently all the way through to the end. And then, at the end, she burst into a short peal of laughter. Sanssouci? Why Sanssouci, of all places? Never mind whether Bach went there, it's like something you'd find in those tacky cover notes they always sell with records! M was at least half joking, but she still sounded somewhat put out. It's true that the place was something of a cliché, a favorite haunt of lovers when they're out for a romantic stroll. In fact, I'd suggested to M that we go and visit the palace that coming summer. The imperfect translation meant my intention hadn't come across particularly well, but in mentioning Sanssouci I'd wanted to express my deep dissatisfaction with reducing such beautiful, meditative music to a mere "offering" to King Frederick. But M shook her head. Music transcends its so-called "creator," rising above whatever motivation—whether individual fame, avarice, or even pure egoism—lay behind its so-called "creation." Music is itself that spirit of artistic creation that can't be compassed by the human, which simply chooses the body of an individual as its temporary vessel. That was M's belief. If that was the case, then dedicating their "own" music to a given individual would be beyond the power of the composer. All the same, I still couldn't bear the fact that Bach had dedicated this wonderful music to King Frederick, any more than if he'd degraded it by an association with the object of some brief, shallow love affair, scrawling a crude dedication: "To the village swine-wench." I refused to tone down these criticisms.

It was a misty morning in early spring, the sky's uniform gray seeming to have become a constant presence in our lives. In the yard belonging to the apartment block, the caretaker's dog was running through the damp grass. Now that we were further into spring, the green light preserved by the woods, the cemetery, the park, and the trees no longer seemed to portend anything in particular. We didn't speak of other things; of Erich, that is, or the future. M seemed depressed. Perhaps it was the fault of the hospital, a place to which M was naturally averse. She'd had her hair cut short during her convalescence, and had taken to wearing a large black hat at all times, refusing to take it off even inside. The slope of her shoulders appeared ever so slightly asymmetrical below its brim. I carried the dining table-cum-desk over to the window and we sat there to drink our tea. M asked when I would be leaving; in two weeks, I replied. She didn't ask when I would be coming back. Instead, she fretted about my accident, when I'd fallen into the water. At the time, when I fell in, I'd felt sure I was going to die, and it still feels like a strange twist of fate that I didn't. It could so easily have proved fatal. I remembered almost nothing about the accident, so was unable to explain to M how such a thing could have happened. M didn't stay long. We were together for an hour and a half, but in all that time we barely spoke, just sat and listened to Mendelssohn. The window looked down onto the paved road, still blanketed with unmelted snow, the yard where the dog tracked back and forth, the bicycle fastened to the iron railing. Rather than destroying the silence inside the house, Mendelssohn's string quartet seemed to exist alongside it. We'd said all we had to say to each other, we'd drunk all the tea, and then the music came to an end. We turned to look at each other as the last notes died away, as though the kitchen was a concert hall, and we were both making sure that the other was ready to get up and leave. M's gaze was steady and direct, without the slightest hint of equivocation. I would have avoided her eyes if I could, but they held me against my will. Looking back on it now, describing those moments when I was unable to tear myself away from M's gaze, I can speak with perfect detachment, even coldly, about how dark and hot it was, stupefying the senses, about that feeling of being deep underwater, cut off, isolated from the world above the surface. Uncompromising, fearless. But there was something else written in M's eyes that day. She was ashamed; ashamed of the crude, underhanded way she'd contributed to ending our relationship, of how, nevertheless, I was the one who'd made a clean break of it, while she found herself unable to let go. That petty sense of shame was the reason M didn't let a single word pass her lips about all that had gone between us, the hope and happiness we'd once shared. She'd overcome it sufficiently to be able to visit me, but it was clearly distressing her the whole time we were together—ashamed of her shame, just as I'd been of mine. It prevented us from being friends, or even strangers. A slave, then, or perhaps just a lookout, a gardener, but no, even that was beyond us. What I saw in M's eyes was blame, anger, disappointment, and worse than all that, the final gestures of despair. I only wish I could say otherwise. When she eventually turned to say goodbye I saw a faint strain of hope materialize in that admixture, a pitiful, weak, selfish kind of hope whose very existence M seemed intending to refute through the cold set of her jaw and the firm line of her mouth. I can't be sure any more, but it's possible that M would have perceived that same hope in my eyes. But though our hands trembled and our ears seemed to pick up the sound of our hearts breaking, not as a clean crack but as a wrenching of fibers, there was still that unaccountable shame over the love that had once existed between us, the fact of this existence now uncomfortably indelible, making the future seem filled with fearful portents. The news came on the radio. M got up from her seat and picked up her crutches and we said a brief goodbye, like people who know they'll be seeing each other again in a few days. I offered to help her to the front door, but she refused. The door closed and left me standing in the hallway, listening to the clumsy, irregular tap of M's crutches as she slowly descended the steps.

If only M had taught me music rather than language. If only I'd been able to perform in front of her, a long stage recital of some string piece I'd learned. If our conversations had revolved around music, rather than language, then I might never have learned anything about her, or the opposite, ended up knowing everything there was to know. She would have been either utterly beyond my grasp, or utterly my possession. The language through which we attempted knowledge of each other was a mere dialect, a mimetic representation of the two entities that were M and myself. Our relationship's reliance on language meant that "I" came to bear less and less resemblance to me, while "M" grew progressively further from M. Had music been our sole means of communication, perhaps things would have turned out differently. The act of its dedication does nothing to music; the music itself remains unchanged. Its value isn't something that can be paid in any other coin, not even with the name of a king. Its blanket forgiveness of human faults is a product of the perfect disregard in which it holds these mere mortals, the immeasurable distance by which it exceeds the minor compass of their lives. Music materializes within these lives, within that roiling mass of pettiness and hunger, greed and want, while at the same time remaining outside, able to fix them with an objective gaze. Or gaze, perhaps, beyond them. "Listening to music" is a rather limited way of describing that self-beholding which human beings can only achieve through the medium of music. Representation—this, after all, is what language and music have in common. Music, though, cannot say all; or even, in fact, anything. Its lips are sealed. Understanding music is not a gradual process. And yet, all of this gets collapsed into that trite expression "listening to music." As M said to me, that time in my rented flat with her own gaze holding me rapt, "Music is the one thing which, of all humans' so-called 'creations,' will never belong to them."

10) As time passed, two opposing desires began to form within me. The first was to carry on as I was, with only my work to occupy my solitary days. I was constantly talking to myself, while I read, while I wrote, while I listened to music, which did away with any need for a social life. It wasn't as though I'd deliberately cloistered myself away when I first came back to Korea, it was simply that I'd lost interest in those acquaintances from my former life. This was a shame, but not something I made any attempt to conceal, so old friends began to distance themselves, leaving me isolated. I was perfectly happy with this state

of affairs. One day I went to the movies with Sumi. The name of the film isn't important, all that matters is that I found it nauseating—not just the film itself, but the whole experience. Even if it had been one of those especially "high-brow" features that do away with all frivolity, coming across as profound and meditative, I doubt whether my reaction would have been any different. Admittedly, the horror I felt as we stood outside the theater wasn't really all that severe, but I couldn't just shrug it off as I would have done in the past, or even put up a fight against it. Of the hordes of people milling around in twos and threes, some were chattering away to their friends, punctuating their conversation with lively gesticulations; others wore smiles of quiet anticipation; others still were stony-faced, their carefully calculated expressions of boredom designed to convey that they had come to see this film quite against their will, that they preferred films of an altogether higher caliber, and though they might fritter away a little time or money on a film like the one they were about to watch, there was absolutely no way they were going to waste any of their precious seriousness on it. Those at the front of the line were being already sucked in to the theater's black interior, but the line still stretched quite a way back, possibly all the way to the nearby subway station. It was strange, but for me there was something deeply unsettling about this long line of people all heading in the same direction. I'd had a similar feeling at other times, and equally keenly, but the incongruity of having it prompted by a theater line, of all things, made it seem ridiculously out of proportion. Even I found something suspicious about it, something stubborn and inexplicable. But I still couldn't shake that sense of unpleasantness. If anything, it was getting stronger. The people in the line weren't pushing and shoving, there was nothing rude in their behavior, nothing repugnant in their appearance, more like the opposite, in fact; their outfits looked perfectly innocuous, and their faces were wreathed in smiles. They were entirely ordinary moviegoers. If it was the case that crowds are always repugnant in and of themselves, then that unpleasantness would have been felt by everyone there, who were as much a part of the crowd as I was. After all, in a huge metropolis like Seoul, it often feels like we're all just a part of one gigantic crowd. But the issue wasn't simply one of quantity. The regimented forward movement, all buoyed by a single aim; the air of anticipation generated by the crowd's volubility; the bright skies and warm sunlight, the neat orderliness of the paving slabs, the smooth-contoured splendor of the building which housed the theater; the fact that this mass convergence of humanity, though an anomaly, still gave off such a luster of organization; the way the film was drawing this crowd toward itself, its influence akin to the way the laws of physics act on dust particles, causing them to coalesce into a single mass; the tempting, honeyed nature of this crowd; these scenes which struck the eye as so ordinary, so animated, so innocent; all of this taken as a whole was so repellent, so frivolous, so unbearably ugly, that it actually caused me physical pain, proof that coming here had been a terrible mistake. Rather than dissipating over the course of the film, this feeling gradually rose to a peak. The images that unfolded on-screen, designed to seem so attractive and tasteful; the impassioned performances, the actors working to convey the very extremes of emotion; the shadowy figures of the audience; the consistent flow of the plot, which never once deviated from the predictable norm; the stultifyingly conventional use of time; the world of the screen, so far removed from that of the written word, its obsessive focus on detail an apparent attempt at exhaustive realism, a realism determined to depict everything "just as it is"; and people, too many people, all those people it aimed to please with its blatant nods and knowing

asides; the experience of actively colluding in the production of
a kind of groupthink, one whose existence nevertheless depends
entirely on this same collective consciousness, without which it
could never have come into being. I sat there, one of the crowd,
struggling to think of a convincing explanation as to why all these
things which, in the past, would have filtered straight through
me and disappeared without a trace, without any of this excessive
repugnance, now felt as stomach-turning as being ambushed in the
street and pelted with sewage. But I just couldn't talk myself out
of it. I couldn't laugh at the obvious puns, or the witty repartee
cleverly inserted at points where the film might otherwise have
threatened to become tedious. Even the big final twist, the hall-
mark of this particular director, did nothing for me. It was all too
repulsive, and I quickly became incredibly distressed. The ordinary
enjoyment of ordinary people, their means of entertainment, the
minutiae of their daily lives, had seemed like nothing so much as
a terrible injustice. "Again I looked and saw all the oppression that
was taking place under the sun . . ."

To a certain extent, Sumi was aware of how the film was affect-
ing me. I clearly hadn't enjoyed myself, at least—I'd sat in silence
the whole time, hadn't laughed or even smiled. But she was patient
with me. When she'd suggested the trip to the movies and asked
what kind of film I'd like to see, I'd told her I didn't care. Now,
she apologized for choosing a film that seemed to have bored me,
though of course none of it was her fault. I explained that it didn't
really matter either way whether the film was boring or not, and
that I hadn't actually found this one particularly tedious, it was
simply an unbearable celebration of the conventional, a sickening
aestheticization of conventional values whose display, moreover,
seemed to form the film's entire basis, and in such a blatant fash-
ion it couldn't help but feel degrading, and finally, that I found it

109

difficult being here, swelling the ranks of the audience for something so flagrantly crass.

Sumi told me I was strange. Rather than agreeing with what I'd said or trying to refute it outright, her chief concern seemed to be bringing me around to her own opinion.

"I'm really sorry if you didn't like the film, but it's not exactly my thing either, you know. I just thought, well, the students are all raving about it, so let's go. If you have that kind of mindset then you can just take it for what it is and not get too serious about it. Films, love, youth—these kinds of things are always going to be 'conventional,' as you put it. Coming to see something conventional, and then complaining that it's conventional, well, isn't that a bit strange?"

"Well, I don't mean that the film itself was particularly, unexpectedly, excessively conventional. What I'm trying to get at, what bothers me, is the whole experience, the event, all these people gathering en masse to have a certain collective image instilled in them, before they all file back out of the building. Somehow I feel damaged by it, though of course that's not your fault, you've done absolutely nothing wrong, so please don't think that's what I'm trying to say. I hope you'll forgive me if I can't explain it properly."

Sumi just sat there and stared at me for a few moments. I was perfectly aware that the film hadn't meant anything special for her. She'd simply wanted a bit of light relaxation, and done nothing more egregious than choose a film that she could sit back and take in with perfect, passive indifference. I would never have said anything about it if she hadn't asked. Now, I couldn't help but worry that I'd made it sound like I was just in a bad mood, my obstinacy no more than the whim of a fractious child. I really hoped I hadn't hurt Sumi, and that my brief explanation had put an end to the whole subject, whether or not it had really succeeded in helping her understand my position. But if she demanded a further explanation then I'd have no choice but to give in, even it meant the risk of digging myself even further into a hole. Otherwise she might end up misunderstanding me completely.

"I never knew you hated films. I mean, you never said anything. If you'd have let me know beforehand then I would have suggested we do something else. I mean, it's fine, anyway. But I've never known anyone with such an aversion to the movies. Why do you hate it so much? Can you explain a bit more?"

"I . . . I don't like all that 'over-accessibility,' you know, things that are deliberately designed to have the broadest possible appeal."

"But making a face and getting into a bad mood just because a film didn't quite agree with you? I really don't mean to criticize, but that's not a very healthy attitude, is it? It doesn't seem very, ah, open-minded. Don't take this the wrong way. It's not that I think you're actually like that, just that your attitude can make it seem . . . oh, you look pale. And you're sweating!"

When I read Shostakovich's memoirs, the part where he describes his childhood stayed with me for a long time. In the introduction he clarifies that, already, these memories of the life he lived are no longer strictly "his," having also been claimed by others. He talks about individuals being reflected in memories and the world at large, and how he himself will live on in this way, through other people's memories, other people's worlds. "Looking back," he says, "I see nothing but ruins, only mountains of corpses." But what made the biggest impression on him wasn't an incident from his childhood, but one in which a talented young film director set a live cow on fire. The director was convinced that this scene, of a cow caught in a conflagration, was absolutely crucial for the film. Eventually, when no one was willing to volunteer, the director decided that he would splash oil over the cow and set it alight himself. He then proceeded to film the crazed beast rampaging about as it burned to death. The director in question was Andrei Tarkovsky. Shostakovich wasn't present at this scene, he only heard the story second-hand, yet even that, he said, was enough to make him feel like he'd been a direct witness to the poor beast's suffering. From his youth, he said, his experience of this world as a place where great numbers of people die utterly senseless deaths had given rise to a phobia regarding the latent tendency toward violence that must exist in such a reality. Consider that cow, he said, burned alive for the sake of art; can such brutal means be justified by the sublimity of the end, by the "genius" of the one who effects them? If so, where does the limit lie? What can compensate for that agony? Is it really possible to hate art, even when that art requires a victim? When suffering is depicted as still more beautiful and genuine for having been deliberately inflicted, can we call that art? Or does the domain of art lie outside that of human experience, human intellect, so that art itself is judged as possessing the strength to transcend universal moral laws? For a long time, Shostakovich's description of that incident with the cow made me doubt the validity of visual art—more concretely, of cinematic art, which functions by effecting a certain emotional response dependent on the apparent "authenticity" of highly manufactured images.

Sumi studied me apprehensively. I had my hands resting on top of the coffee table; she reached out and covered them with hers. I was surprised, even a little flustered. Sumi wasn't the type for public displays of affection. Her hands were surprisingly warm, her fingers long and slender, her palms soft. Though relatively young, she was mature and levelheaded. She wasn't particularly fond of things like books or music, which to her were passive objects of consumption, but was perfectly able to hold her own in a conversation on literary or musical subjects. She was always immaculately turned out, too; yet while outwardly she was all studied elegance, inwardly she was kind and unpretentious. Her interests were varied and seemingly endless: Greenpeace, animal conservation, pacifism, veganism (she wouldn't even add milk to her coffee), Tibetan Buddhism, playing the balalaika, Siberia, the abolition of capital punishment, support groups for lesbian mothers. Sumi's parents, one Swiss and one Korean, had raised her with a deep understanding of each of their respective cultures, and the advantages of this wide cultural grounding could be seen in all manner of instances. Take the film we'd seen that day, which Sumi had been far better able to tolerate, understand, and even enjoy than had I, a full-blooded Korean. There were some who found her combination of prudence and intelligence, all wrapped up in stylish elegance, extremely alluring. But that day at the theater, standing by the coffee table in the lobby and discussing our responses, I slowly became aware that the specific object of my displeasure was none other than Sumi herself. Not because she'd been the one to choose that film, and not because any specific thing she'd said or done had upset me. According to her, she'd found the film every bit as meaningless as I had, though she'd at least managed to get some level of enjoyment from it. It seemed unfair to criticize her. She'd only acted in accordance with her nature, which was to always look for the positives in every situation, to accept her everyday environment for what it was. Sumi was adept at swimming with the current, at getting what she needed from whatever was given her to work with. Objective observation revealed that none of her attributes were inherent. Whether it was her intellect or her sense of style, Sumi absorbed as much as possible from those around her, figuring out and then putting into practice the things she learned at school, in a meeting, in whatever company she was in. Outwardly, she seemed healthy, firm, and fair. But that was only outwardly. She tended to be indifferent toward anything that, for whatever reason, wasn't illuminated by the glare of mass-media attention, or didn't give the observer an immediate visual kick. You mightn't have known it from the uniform goodwill she displayed toward even these less glamorous causes, but inside they left her cold. The real issue, perhaps, was that everything Sumi knew or believed, she'd learned from the media. She could only ever get excited about a given cause if it came packaged with an air of tragedy or altruism. Her passion for such things was as much a part of her style as her precisely planned outfits, the product of Sumi's letting herself be led by her least refined self. She was always full of explanations and excuses, citing so-called 'just causes' and 'humanist conscience,' which couldn't help but seem over the top, as though she was seeking to elevate her interests with the gloss of high seriousness. She had no qualms whatsoever about sullying the term "revolution" by associating it with some of the most pointless junk churned out by the twenty-first century, on the contrary, she got a real kick out of it. She comprised her own world, single and self-contained, just as a person huddling rapt in front of their television set seems to be opening themselves up to the world on its screen, while in reality remaining completely isolated. Sumi herself, in other words, was akin to this audiovisual transmitter of isolation, the dark underbelly of the image world, that destructive force going by the name of public fraternity. She made a clear distinction between things that appealed to her and those that didn't, elevating the former by granting them use of the name "just cause." Her ostensible fight was against the various forms of irrational violence in the world, but of course her main incentive was to appeal to the general majority, making herself into someone who would capture the hearts of these innumerable strangers, or at least imitating such a person, acquiring for herself that power, both material and immaterial, to command others' emotions, which is such a valuable commodity within society. Sumi's many "causes" had no value for her when taken on their own, only as instances of a certain model or type which exists as an abstract grouping, like Hello Kitty merchandise. As soon as all of this became clear to me, my feelings toward her rapidly cooled. That day at the movies, Sumi ceased, for me, to be a distinct individual, her features blurring as she melted back in to the crowd. Admittedly, this caused me a brief pang of guilt, but nothing more serious than that. Sumi was innocent, pure as a lamb, but when all was said and done she was just another one of the crowd. In aligning themselves with the tastes and inclinations of the masses, the many facets of her appeal, whose precise function was to capture people's attention, lost any appeal they might have had for me. I couldn't stand the masses any more, couldn't stand the theaters which housed them or the films which sought to please them, and couldn't stand Sumi, for whom all of these things weren't sickening but somehow, incomprehensibly, a source of enjoyment. Sumi isn't one of a kind. The masses are made up of innumerable Sumis. And so, if I can't stand Sumi as a non-specific noun, what this really amounts to is that I can't stand any of you. And neither did I hide this feeling.

115

The second desire was to see M. I was well aware that she probably wasn't M any more, that this M wasn't the M I'd once loved, but still I searched for her, I missed her. Perhaps, I thought, she might appear in some other form. To my shame, I have to confess that I once mistook Sumi for M. Sumi's fresh scent, exuding an air of health; the intimacy in her gaze when our eyes first met and she, instead of looking away, came forward to examine me more closely;

the way her back curved down from those beautiful high shoulders, I'd always liked women who managed to look healthy as a mare despite having tall, elegant frames. Affable Sumi, who could converse easily on all manner of topics, yet remained stubbornly closed to debate when it came to her personal tastes, really had deserved the nickname "my beautiful *mischling*." Later, though, I realized that this wasn't enough for me to confuse Sumi with M. M was never going to charm someone at a first meeting, whatever beauty and virtues she possessed weren't the kind to be easily recognizable. If they had been, she wouldn't have been M. M wasn't someone whose entire being could be summed up in a snappy slogan or TV debate. Rather, she was like a book without any pictures. In other words, the kind of person who, unless you brought your whole soul to bear in reading them, would remain forever unknowable. I couldn't come to terms with the fact that I would never see M again in this life, that I'd lost that opportunity forever. The pain of her absence never lessened. If it had, there would have been nothing driving me out into the streets, compelling me to scan those countless faces for a glimpse of familiarity, to walk up to total strangers and address them, listening intently to catch every inflection of their reply. Without the hope of finding M again, would I ever have gotten to know Sumi? For a long time I was obsessed by the thought that M was there, somewhere, the thought of her eyes as we'd said our final farewell, the thought that they might captivate me once again. Surely, I thought, it was just a matter of knowing where to look. Only it seemed, in the end, I never did.

11) The sequence of past, present, and that time we call the future, exists in this successive form only as it appears to the eye. Such a sequence has no real existence in our mental

world. The only thing that truly communicates real, intimate existence to us is the fact that, strictly speaking, the present does not exist. Time becomes a stale model of itself, mutually penetrating and acting. It is plural and multi-level. This is the point of departure for all my thoughts on music.

Bernd Alois Zimmerman's final composition was a religious one; in *Requiem for a Young Poet* of 1969, he quotes from the book of Ecclesiastes: "Again I looked and saw all the oppression that was taking place under the sun." This quotation claims to transcribe the words of Solomon; the passage from which it is taken is filled with pessimism regarding the mortal world. "Again I looked and saw all the oppression that was taking place under the sun. I saw the tears of the oppressed—and they have no comforter; power was on the side of their oppressors—and they have no comforter. And I declared that the dead, who had already died, are happier than the living, who are still alive. But better than both is the one who has never been born, who has not seen the evil that is done under the sun." The piece begins with a solemn, weighty voice, followed by two vocalists, a bass solo, and then the orchestra. As well as the passage from Ecclesiastes, some lines from Dostoevsky's *The Brothers Karamazov* are also quoted. Until I attended "A Night of Russian Literature and Music" at a music school, I'd never heard of Bernd Alois Zimmerman. And even if I had, it would have been as just one more name to add to the list of twentieth-century composers whose works I hadn't heard or were still not widely known, yet were quite skilled or at least said to be, like Wolfgang Rihm, Franz Schreker, John Cage, Pierre Boulez, or Yun Isang.

Going to the concert hall where the music is actually performed, brought to life in front of you, is a unique and mysterious experience, one that sets your pulse fluttering. At the same time, though, it's also an uneasy one, accompanied beforehand by chest-tightening anxiety, your nerves strained to the breaking point as you hesitate over whether to attend the recital. All recitals, without exception, can be classified as one of two types: popular, well-known musicians, performing in a large venue; or unknowns whose talent is still up for debate. With the former, there's a higher likelihood of encountering music in its perfected form, but you have to be willing to risk those countless annoyances that are a feature of any crowd, and which could severely impair your enjoyment of the performance: endless coughing; vigorous, impatient rustling sounds; loud whispers from the audience; the inevitable ring of a mobile phone; nervous fidgeting; and then, of course, there's the packed cafeteria, the difficulty of booking in advance, the fear you can never quite shake that, when the pianist's fingers linger on a certain chord, somehow managing to draw out the notes' reverberations for so long it seems like magic, and you unwittingly hold your breath so as not to break the spell, that splendid, incomparable perfection might suddenly be destroyed by an explosive noise from the audience. Your already-keen hearing becomes even more acute, and you end up concocting scenarios in which, quite apart from any audience interruptions, the music itself can't be heard properly even from the best seats in the venue, and you start fretting over the concert hall's layout and acoustics, wondering whether the seat you've chosen is really at the ideal angle to the stage or whether you ought to try a different one, whether the piano or P. A. system will be up to scratch or whether there'll be unwanted vibrations, and you start to regard the performer with a critical gaze, finding fault with this and that, making comparisons, ranking this performance against others you've attended, assessing in which aspect this performer appears preeminent and in which another is superior, an endless stream of almost hostile criticisms serving solely for the

118

critic to parade their own taste, and, finally, stooping so far that you even start making arrogant, snobbish pronouncements regarding the architecture and acoustics. In reality, these desperate efforts to get the best out of a performance paradoxically end up making music's suitors—whose amateur hearts love timidly and secretly—fear to set foot in the concert hall. Of course, if you're lucky then you'll leave the performance suffused with private joy at the beauty of the music, a feeling entirely unsullied by any other considerations. But with celebrated performers, those media darlings who can boast of countless prizes and glittering careers, there's always a greater likelihood of being dissatisfied, either with the performance itself or with all those various attendant factors. This said, it's still possible to come across performers who feel that their fame brings with it a certain responsibility, who've learned to live with that fame so that it doesn't detract from their art, and it's one of the greatest joys there is when you do. And it wasn't just the performers I got to know through attending recitals; they also afforded me the opportunity to re-encounter certain modern composers who, up until then, I'd never really understood and therefore hadn't been able to appreciate properly. This is the main reason that I continue going to concerts, in spite of the manifold awkwardness involved. Otherwise, I would never have had the marvelous experience of encountering the music of Liszt and Chopin anew, which I'd listened to now and then from quite a young age, but always without interest. Likewise with Béla Bartók and Bernd Alois Zimmerman. But there's a different, simpler joy in attending smaller, simpler recitals. For one, you can arrive at the venue quite naturally, a solitary individual out for a walk, rather than feeling that you've been pulled there by that tensile strength which moves a huge crowd. These performances don't always satisfy those who have a finely tuned ear for music, and you're unlikely to encounter new musicians in a new way. But there's more than enough value to be found in a Bach concert one evening, the interior of the church strafed with the late autumn light; a cello recital held in the reception area of a concert hall rather than one of its main auditoria; a piano quintet; a piece by a music school graduate, based around two violins and a computer, which is extremely experimental and completely does away with melody; aspiring young musicians; people who have a clear idea of what they love; the fortuitous pleasure of stumbling across a string quartet whom you'd previously heard in much grander settings, with their stylish interpretation of Shostakovich. Such occasions put you in a comfortable, indulgently receptive state of mind, like an evening walk over a carpet of fallen leaves, freeing you from considerations of fame and sharp tongues, giving you space to reflect on yourself and the world, to forget the complications and insecurities caused by the critic who lurks in the mind's dark places. "A Night of Russian Literature and Music" was no different. The venue was a crowded building on a wealthy residential street; I'd missed the city circle bus as I didn't have a copy of the timetable, so I'd had to walk from the subway station, quite a long way, and this was after ten at night. But I wasn't the least bit afraid, although I was alone. I heard dogs barking now and then, but I never saw another person. Whenever I turned a corner or came to a small crossroads I would unfold my map under the faint glow from the street lights and find the name of the street I was on, those still, nocturnal streets, smothered in silence, against which my footsteps or the crunch of leaves was startlingly loud, as I wandered around looking for the white signboards on which the house numbers were written. And it was Bernd Alois Zimmerman that my journey brought me to. It was past midnight when I made my way back, and of course there was no-one else about, the night was cold, the woods by the side of the road were black and the wind scraped past my ears, but I walked along half in a daze, alive to nothing but the music I'd just heard. When those who have given everything they had to and in service of music sense the approach of death, when death cannot but become their theme and they themselves cannot but confess its omnipotence, and death becomes the summation of life; the first time I recognized music created in such a moment was when I heard Shostakovich's final sonata. It was only later that I read about his contradictory life, the life of someone who, though renowned and successful, a celebrity among the privileged classes of the former USSR, had at the same time been a puppet, a lonely individual insulted and ridiculed at the whim of the masses. That same day, I listened again to Zimmerman's last two compositions. Though the quotations were taken from a religious text, their significance wasn't limited to the sphere of religion. I suspected that Zimmerman wasn't religious in the usual sense of the word, rather that for him it was all the same whether he was quoting religious texts, Bach's cantata or the Grand Inquisitor's speech. Because, after all, his final work was a way of announcing his imminent departure from this world. Five days after "Again I looked and saw . . ." was completed, Bernd Alois Zimmerman committed suicide. We're told that he suffered from severe depression.

When I got back to Seoul my financial situation was much worse than I'd thought. My bank balance had long since hit rock bottom, there was absolutely no possibility of my finding any other source of income and, on top of that, the rent had been pushed up by the skyrocketing value of real estate. I had to abandon for good the idea I'd had of wintering in Norway or Finland. When I'd first mentioned the thought to M or Joachim they'd tried to dissuade me from such a foolish undertaking, but it had been a long-held dream of mine to sit out the winter in some snow-bound northern port town. I sold my car, but this was no great help. My relatives lent me some money in exchange for the use of my house. It wasn't enough—no, to be frank the whole situation was horribly uncertain—but all the same it was helpful when it came to writing, because I ended up even less attached to my present self. I'd encountered Zimmerman at exactly the right time, because just then, as he puts it, the definite "present" didn't strictly exist for me. I'd simply stopped for a while in a certain fluid place between past and future, these two states giving direction to my present situation, and through writing I would reappear as myself in given moments from the past or future. This is how I thought of M. Inside me M was already dead, and the thought of her no longer caused me any sadness or anger. If anything, I felt closer to her. Representing her like this, as someone who may or may not exist, ultimately became my reason to write. Rather than there being any sense of loss or fulfillment, this was an anaesthetized, factual, dispassionate state of affairs. I forgot the time and place I was in.

Or perhaps I began to write this piece at a certain place that winter. There's a strong possibility that it began as a letter to M. Only while it was still possible, in my mind if nowhere else, for me to write something to M did my desk, the potential site of such an act, seem the most wondrous spot on this earth. And while I was writing I acted as though entirely oblivious to the disappearance of all that had once existed between M and I, a way for me to forget my own forgetfulness, and gain some measure of solace. In order to forget my sadness, I had to forget that I'd already stopped being sad. As I begin to write, I experience the same heavy languor, the same unplaceable sense of loss, and of illusoriness of all things, as when I wake from a long afternoon nap. The soft, far-off light of evening, making a pale square of the window in the unlit room; the hard wooden chair and desk, the empty room. I walk over to the desk. The dreams that reveal me for what I am still linger, though my waking self has already forgotten them. Now is the time of the setting sun, blazing in the sky above the darkness of the earth. The time when things have individual voices, and speak to me. Relying on the last light of the evening sky, I begin to write.

One day a letter came from Joachim, saying he hoped I could stay at his house over January and look after Benny while he took a trip to Schleswig-Holstein. And that if I wanted to take a break from work I should come with him on his trip. I recalled how the idea of traveling north always used to have such a hold on me. My default response was one of apathy, and I drafted a letter of refusal. From a certain point onward, I'd stopped wanting to go anywhere at all. But I soon changed my mind.   *123*

12) Now, to put it as Kundera might, we enter a secret world, populated by a cast of nameless characters. It is a kind of dream world. Hunger, disease, confusion, separation, curses, forgetfulness, ignorance and superficiality, all human suffering is there in that world just as it ever was, only now it no longer has a name. My walks gradually lengthened as January came to an end, eventually taking me all the way to Cité Foch and the edge of the lake. Cité Foch was the area where French officers had lived after the war, and had retained the atmosphere of a small, self-contained city within a city. You could still come across street signs for Rue Racine and Rue Diderot. But by then, aside from several restaurant signs in French, it wasn't all that different from other areas on the edges of the city center. The sun had yet to go down,

but the day was dark. The gloaming, a dark gold like the old light of a forest's inner fastness, hung suspended over streets, houses and roads, over a small stream which flowed out of the woods and into a canal. Pink clouds shimmered on one edge of the sky. But the darkness, washed in strong red light, robbed all earthly things of their true form, their self-assurance. An abandoned railway lay at the edge of the woods, its tracks overgrown with dried grasses. Warehouses barricaded with enormous padlocks, gardens that had been left to go to seed, and vacant lots piled high with abandoned goods, flanked both sides. The dirt road leading into the woods was churned up with snowmelt. Dried vines that had sprouted up haphazardly were straggling over the timbered walls enclosing the vacant lot. The musty smell of damp was faintly discernible, as was the metallic tang of gasoline. There was a motorway nearby. It wasn't the kind of place that anyone would call a beautiful spot for a walk. That place, where no one lived any more, was desolate. Here and there in the distance you could make out the rectangular forms of yellow-daubed apartment buildings, but they looked strangely sullen squatting there in the gathering dark, as if all life within them had died. The path was hard to make out among the snow and grass and fallen leaves, and I frequently stumbled. After a while, I came to the place where the railway ended. The path had been blocked off; there was no way to go any further. M might still have been living in Cité Foch for all I knew, but then again she might not. She might just as easily have been ill. In any case, it wasn't thoughts of M that had brought me there. I'd changed at Alexanderplatz to whichever tram had been going furthest out of the city, and it was entirely by coincidence that the tram happened to be going to Cité Foch. I stayed on the path until night had completely fallen. The clouds glided apart, revealing the huge red disc of the moon. On the main road, the late-opening cafés were packed with customers, raucous with music and laughter. At the Mexican restaurant on the corner the staff were barbecuing in the yard. The faces visible through the frosted glass window were flushed with excitement. The candlelit tables were overflowing with plates of food and teacups, cigarettes and wine glasses. Eventually I discovered an empty seat, in a café on the corner, sat down and ordered coffee with a tomato and mozzarella sandwich. The interior was humid, a thick fug of cigarette smoke, and felt chilly despite all the customers. Those sitting near me were all drinking beer, their high-pitched voices rattling on without a pause, and gesticulating so wildly they sometimes found themselves half out of their seats. The waitress weaved skillfully between them with her tray, shouting out so they wouldn't knock into her, these people going to the bathroom or to buy cigarettes or simply wandering about drunk on conversation. Through the window I could see the last lingering light from the setting sun, scarring the black sky as sharply as knife wounds. It's the only light that comes from the earth, rather than being suspended from some overhead canopy; it knows no hesitation or guilty conscience, and its red majesty brings your heart close to bursting, boring into you like a unique epiphany. Like something that will not come again; like something that will not come twice, that is. That winter evening of deserted roads, with the snow still lying on the ground but with another blizzard yet to come, I sat at a small, one-person table in front of a window that seemed it would never be clean, and grew slowly faint, receding into the glass. After drinking the coffee and eating the sandwich I, nameless I, went and got on the tram, let it take me away from that place. It was the only time I ever visited Cité Foch.

I opened the door and entered the room. M was standing by the desk. The light slanted in through the window, so that M's figure was half illuminated by golden light and half sunk in shade. As soon as she saw me she strode forward, hand outstretched. We shook hands, and M introduced herself: "M."

We went over to the sofa and sat down. M was wearing a gray wool skirt and a pullover with lots of folds at the neckline. A black leather belt encircled her waist. Only when she shifted a little closer to me could I see her face in detail. My first thought was of how pale she was, and that I'd never seen such a strikingly androgynous face. Our eyes met. I wanted to look away, but couldn't.

"First I want to hear what your reading's like. Could you read for me? Any page, and take your time."

M went to the bookcase, swiftly brushed her fingers over the spines, extracted one of the volumes and brought it over to me. I couldn't understand the words on the cover. I opened it somewhere in the middle and tried to read. The page I'd opened it on had a black and white photograph of a man with glasses and a beard. To me he looked like a doctor, a journalist, perhaps a physics teacher.

"The sequence of past, present, and . . . that time we call the future, exists in this . . . successive form only as . . . it appears . . . to the eye."

After stumbling through that first sentence, I looked at M. My eyes said: I should stop here, right? That sentence was completely incomprehensible to me.

M's eyes said: Why did you stop?

"I don't understand what these words mean."

"Even if you can't understand, you can still make me understand. Look at it that way, and as time passes you'll come to understand it too. Are you thinking of taking formal lessons?"

I shook my head. And continued, as best I could, to read.

"Such a sequence has no real existence in our mental world. The only thing that truly communicates real, intimate existence to us is the fact that, strictly speaking, the present does not exist. Time becomes a stale model of itself . . ."

I closed the book. Aside from some basic verbs, the whole thing remained an enigma, and I couldn't help but think that this was a rather unwise and ineffective method of teaching. M remained perfectly silent, waiting for me to either continue reading, or else put the book down and leave. We sat there and looked at each other. M was never the type to break my heart. If such a type had existed, that is. But there was something about M that aroused my curiosity, which set her apart, permeating her movements, her gaze, her attitude. Something in her nature awakened both compassion and the desire to be overpowered, revealing a freely willed carnal desire and, at the same time, the spontaneous restriction of this will. She'd clearly been living on her own for some time, relying only on her own standards. Even while doubting the validity of her teaching method, I was slowly drawn to M. This bafflement and uncertainty was all there in my expression, plain to see. But M's apparent composure never faltered. Later, though, she confessed that she too had been seized by an awful trembling, which she'd had to clench both hands to suppress, and had even sensed that we would end up having an intimate connection. Sitting up straight and with her hands resting on her knees, her posture never changing, M finished the sentence from where I left off.

". . . mutually penetrating and acting."

I remember the Icelandic girl I met when I visited the Zwinger, a little while before returning to Korea. She was short, and wore her hair in the cropped style popular among teachers. She came straight up to me and, without any preamble (and in really elegant English), asked my name. Bundled up in a black wool coat, she looked cold, and seemed somewhat naive. She genuinely wanted to know my name. Apparently she thought I might be an ex-girlfriend of hers, whom she'd broken up with several years ago. This was all she said, so I wasn't sure whether she meant there was some facial resemblance, or if there was some other reason making her think I might be the ex-girlfriend she'd lost. I also didn't know what country her ex-girlfriend was from; the only thing I knew for certain was that she wasn't me. I'd never met this Icelandic woman before. She was almost certainly going to be disappointed when I told her my name. There was absolutely no way that she was M. But then, how can we ever really expect to be completely certain about what a person is? When I eventually told her my name she made a face and, looking resentful, turned and walked back across the palace yard, which had a thin crust of ice, flouncing away like a schoolgirl. Why can't she remember her own ex-girlfriend's face properly? She doesn't recognize me; I mean, what real meaning is there in a name, which is merely an optional identifier? Might she have been M after all?

At my desk I continue to write. As Peter Handke says, "Only when I'm writing do I feel that I've become myself and am truly at home." Where it comes from and where it goes, on that its lips are sealed.

Bae Suah, one of the most highly acclaimed contemporary Korean authors, has published more than a dozen works and won several prestigious awards. She has also translated several books from the German, including works by W. G. Sebald, Franz Kafka, and Jenny Erpenbeck. Her first book to appear in English, *Nowhere to be Found*, was longlisted for a PEN Translation Prize and the Best Translated Book Award.

Deborah Smith's literary translations from the Korean include two novels by Han Kang (*The Vegetarian* and *Human Acts*), and two by Bae Suah (*A Greater Music* and *Recitation*). She also recently founded Tilted Axis Press to bring more works from Africa, Asia, and the Middle East into English.

**OPEN
LETTER**

**OPEN
LETTER**